THE
SAINTS
ALSO GET SICK

RALPH CULP

PAGE PUBLISHING, INC.
Conneaut Lake, PA

First originally published by Page Publishing 2021

Scripture quotations are from the following versions:
Authorized King James Version—KJV.

Scripture quotations marked NLT are taken from the Holy Bible,
New Living Translation, copyright 1996, 2004. Used by permission
of Tyndale House Publishers, Inc. Carol Stream, Illinois 60188.

ISBN 978-1-6624-2870-8 (pbk)
ISBN 978-1-6624-2871-5 (digital)

Printed in the United States of America

Contents

Introduction

In THE YEAR 2000, my wife was diagnosed with ovarian cancer. Becky was a healthy, energetic lady. As a professional hairdresser, she often worked long hours. We loved to travel and use vacation times camping. She could stir up a frittata for breakfast on the campfire that would melt in your mouth!

She began noticing a lack of energy and grew tired before the day ended. There was a sudden weight gain and swelling from retained fluids. She suffered severe abdominal pains.

Her primary doctor recommended extensive testing. The results of the tests were not good. The attending physician at the hospital was a young resident. He sat beside her on the bed and spoke with compassion, "I have the worst news anyone can hear. The X-rays show numerous tumors. The T cell count in your blood should be an average of three to five; yours is over three hundred. This indicates cancer. I will locate a cancer specialist who can see you immediately!"

This news came on Friday. The doctor had her set for an appointment the following Monday with the West Cancer Clinic in Memphis, Tennessee. The diagnosis was a fourth stage ovarian cancer. It had metastasized throughout her abdomen. The doctors indicated at this stage and severity, six months would be a long time for life. They offered one option: radical surgery followed by extensive chemotherapy treatments. This, they said, could extend her life for possibly two years.

Becky's dad had died at age fifty-two with pancreatic cancer. She had watched him struggle and understood what the months ahead held for her. There was disappointment in her face but a victorious faith in her heart. Never at any time did she bemoan her fate.

A well-intentioned friend asked, "Becky, do you not feel this is so unfair? You inspire and help so many. Why would God allow this to happen to you? Have you not asked, 'Lord, why me?'"

Becky's response to that question is the basis for this writing.

She answered, "No, but I have asked, 'Why not me?' I am not immune to sickness just because I am Christian. This cancer may end in death, but for now, it is just a part of my living!"

The following pages are devotional Bible studies designed to help us understand more completely that *The Saints Also Get Sick!*

SICKNESS AND SUFFERING

THE NORMAL RESPONSE to sickness is to seek the advice of a doctor. Too often we allow an uncomfortable condition to persist until the gnawing pains can be tolerated no longer. At the clinic we explain, "'Doc, I don't feel so well! What is wrong with me?"

We are sure the doctor can accurately diagnose the problem and prescribe a magic potent for an instant relief. In order to give an accurate diagnosis, the doctor must know prevailing symptoms so he asks, "How long have you felt this way? Any chills or fever? Nausea or headaches? How is your appetite? Are you sleeping?"

It is important that the doctor know the medical history so the patient may be asked to complete a medical record. A diagnosis may be impossible to know until certain tests are completed. Scans and X-rays, blood tests, and a complete examination will give the doctor a thorough understanding of the illness and its treatment.

An accurate diagnosis is imperative before proper treatments and medicines can be administered.

> The Ole Doc is weird and a little crazy I fear,
> For when I said my tummy aches,
> he looked inside my ear!

He listened to me when I coughed,
and when I sneezed "A-Choo,"
He took my temp and felt my
pulse and ran a test or two.
"I don't know what it is you've got,
but I do know what it's not...
It's not your heart and not your
head. It's not your back or knee!
Your pains will become more
severe once you get my fee!"

—Ralph Culp

In the following devotions, we seek for a biblical diagnosis to better understand why *The Saints Also Get Sick!*

The Chaos of Suffering

"Oh, Woe Is Me!"

"And now my life seeps away. Depression haunts my days. At night my bones are filled with pain, which gnaws at me relentlessly ... My heart is troubled and restless. Days of suffering torment me... My skin is turned dark, and my bones bum with fever. And I know you [God] are sending me to my death—the destination of all who live" (Job 30:16–17, 27, 30, 23 NLT).

Three o'clock in the morning, everyone was asleep. The night was still and quiet, but inside my body Mount St. Helens was about to erupt! The gurgling and rumbling coming from my abdomen was crying loud and clear, "Get to the bathroom ASAP!"

It was not a pretty sight. I felt weak and dizzy. The room was spinning around me, and everything went dark! The cool tile floor of the bathroom became my bed for the rest of the night. I felt comforted with the commode at my fingertips.

The next morning, I was pale and pathetically helpless. My muscles ached. My joints were stiff; I could hardly move, and all I could say was "Oh, woe is me!" I was helped to the car and transported to the nearest urgent care clinic. A sympathetic nurse soothed my nerves as well as my medical needs.

The nurse advised that plenty of liquids, no solid foods, and rest would take care of the problem. She diagnosed it well. In less than twenty-four hours, I was as good as new. Where did I get this nauseating nuisance? Had I been bitten by a rabid raccoon? Did I drink contaminated water? Had I been exposed to toxic waste or asbestos poisoning? No, a simple stomach virus put me to my knees.

Amazing, isn't it? These bodies can be trained to withstand the elements of nature on a trek up Mt. Everest. We may push to the limits in a "strong man" marathon or submit to rigorous "jungle warfare" training without a hitch. Then a simple little virus germ can put us to bed writhing in pain and begging for mercy!

Why do we suffer? What causes our sicknesses? Why do we have pains and problems, hurts and heartaches, weaknesses and woes? Job cried in the midst of his torments, "Oh, Woe is me!"

A counselor advises that you are tired, overworked, and just experiencing burnout. The doctor may suspect your immune system is weakened. The psychologist indicates you are anxious and frustrated. The dietitian advises that you are not eating proper food for healthy nourishment and adequate vitamin intake.

A genetics specialist advises that the problem is in your genes. Your grandfather had this problem. Your father has this problem. Now you have this problem! Everyone seems to have an answer, yet we are still confused, in chaos, as to the "why" of human suffering. Since God is the creator of life and formed man's body, his Word on the cause and effect of suffering is definite and final.

Man is a mixture, a composite of the physical, emotional, and spiritual. The Apostle Paul reminds us, "And the very God of peace sanctify you wholly, and I pray God your whole spirit and soul and body be preserved (1 Thessalonians 5:23 KJV).

Pain, suffering, and sorrows are potholes in the pavement on the road of life. The body will succumb to disease. The mind may experience mental fatigue resulting in forgetfulness or much more severe psychosis. Emotionally, we may give way to a "nervous breakdown" or to seasons of depression.

Each area of life is affected by the whole of life as though interwoven together. The wisdom of the Proverbs states, "…A broken heart crushes the spirit… For the despondent, every day brings trouble… But a broken spirit saps a person's strength" (Proverbs 15:13, 15; 17:22 NLT).

Ills and woes are suffered in various levels of intensity in each part of our delicate makeup. For instance, severe pain or extended suffering in the body wears on the nerves. Nervousness leads to anxiety. Anxiety gives way to fear and depression. In a state of depression, a person may neglect or abuse his body to compensate for the emotional trauma he is experiencing. Other complicated problems are soon to develop. Life is like a broken record; it keeps repeating itself. This vicious cycle will spiral out of control unless the ailing person seeks medical attention or counseling.

The patriarch Job, enduring a test of faith, experienced almost every physical and emotional ailment known to his generation. He signified his symptoms and specified his diagnosis. He felt a sense of comfort in knowing that this is the journey and the destination of all mankind on the earth. So he declares, "Man that is born of woman is of few days and full of trouble. He comes forth like a flower and is cut down; he flees also as a shadow and continues not" (Job 14:1–2).

The cycle of being human—man—born of woman—few days—full of trouble includes suffering and survival, sickness and health, joys and sorrows, victories and losses, crowns and crosses. No one is exempt. Even Jesus suffered. "And he began to teach them, that the Son of man must suffer many things…and be killed…" (Mark 8:31 KJV). The saints also get sick! "Yet if any man suffer as a Christian, let him not be ashamed; but let him glorify God on this behalf" (1 Peter 4:16 KJV).

Suffering is a *normal* occurrence. The human body is a weaving of muscle and nerves stretched over a framework of bones and joints, held together by ligaments and cartilages. The nervous system, the body's pain center, acts as a messenger to notify the outer extremities that something is wrong. "Ouch, that hurts!" is our response to mashing a finger or stubbing a toe. Without pain, we would be zombies. Pain is therefore normal to these bodies.

Suffering is a *natural* experience. From the womb to the tomb, man is tormented and afflicted. There is pain associated with birth. Eve was informed that giving birth would be painful. "I will sharpen the pain of your pregnancy, and in pain you will give birth" (Genesis 3:16 NLT). "A woman when she is in travail hath sorrow, because her hour is come: but as soon as she is delivered of the child, she remembereth no more the anguish, for joy that a man is born into the world" (John 16:21 KJV).

There is pain associated with living. The terms "labor" and "sorrow" and" travail" are used extensively throughout the Bible to identify pains and misery associated with living. "Every man is paralyzed with fear. Every heart melts, and people are terrified. "Pangs of anguish grip them, like those of a woman in labor" (Isaiah 13:8 NLT).

Life is often consumed with various illnesses, infirmities, injuries, and impairments. The very process of growing up and growing older is saturated with varying levels of painful problems associated with age and development. Youth may experience muscle cramps often referred to as "growth pains." A senior adult may experience a lapse in memory or momentary confusion. These emotional traumas may be diagnosed as "sundown syndrome."

One could easily say, "Well, that's just life!"

There is suffering associated with healing. "A certain woman, which had an issue of blood twelve years, and had suffered many things of many physicians, and had spent all that she had, and was nothing bettered, but rather grew worse" (Mark 5:25–26 KJV).

Only a recovering cancer patient knows the depth of anguish and suffering associated with chemotherapy or radiation treatments. A person may lose weight, lose their hair, lose muscle tone and strength, lose an appetite for eating, develop allergic reactions to treatments, and become medicine-dependent for the remainder of life in order to prolong their days with hope of enjoying life once again.

There is pain associated with death. In 1846, John Quincy Adams suffered a stroke. When asked by a friend of his health, he answered, "I inhabit a weak, frail, decayed tenement; battered by the winds and broken in upon by the storms, and, from all I can learn, the landlord does not intend to repair."

Modern medical advancements have made death and dying more humane. Hospice palliative care and the use of pain-reducing medications make dying easier to accept and experience.

Suffering is an *expected* occurrence. When someone is involved in an accident, our immediate response is, "Are you hurt?" No matter what may occur, if one slips on the icy walkway or cuts a finger peeling potato or bumps his head on the door, some level of pain is expected. We look at the mangled wreckage of an automobile where the driver walked away uninjured and respond, "Wow! That is amazing! You could have been hurt!"

Pain and suffering are expected entities in life. We approach many of life's experiences with an anticipation of pain to follow. At the health clinic, the little fellow about to receive his flu vaccine whines, "It's gonna hurt!" At the health spa, an overweight participant begs off from the exercises. "These sit-ups are too much for me. My back will start hurting again!" The instructor quips back, "Remember, no pain, no gain!"

Sickness, suffering, and death are normal, natural, and expected experiences in life. How beautiful the thought that in all of life's trials and triumphs, God's presence will comfort, control, and bring cheer to the believer. "Yea, though I walk through the valley of the shadow of death, I will fear no evil: for thou art with me..." (Psalm 23:4 KJV). Wow, what a wonderful experience: valleys, shadows, evils but no fear! Why? God is walking us through these valleys.

We are never alone, nor do we get lost in the darkness!

The Classroom of Suffering

"The School of Hard Knocks!"

"Why am I discouraged? Why is my heart so sad? I will put my hope in God! I will praise him again—my Savior and my God!" (Psalm 43:5 NLT).

This prayer of the psalmist has been echoed often by the saints. This plaintive plea, a compassionate complaint is "Lord, why this dark valley?" "Why is this happening to me?" "Lord, where are you? I need you today!"

Life is full of various and variegated experiences. Some are good and exciting times. Others are sad and fearful times. We can cry because roses have thorns, or we can celebrate that thorns have roses. Mostly everyone has at some time in their life questioned the experiences which they face. Many have doubted God's hand at work in the urgent and ugly times. Grieved and wounded souls cry for mercy. Even the Lord Jesus cried out from the cross, "Why hast thou forsaken me?" (Matthew 27:46 KJV).

Who among us has not at some time thought that "life is not fair" or asked "Does God even care?" In our "feeling sorry for myself" moments we make comparisons of ourselves to others. We take note of their prosperity and feel the plight of our poverty. We grudge their gains as we loathe our lack. We say to ourselves, "I don't understand. I go to church, pray, tithe, love my neighbor, and teach my children to do right, but what do I get from it? I see people living horrible lives and never pray or go to church, and they are so blessed? Lord, why?"

The psalmist David in observing life often cried over the inequities of his existence. "For I envied the proud when I saw them prosper despite their wickedness. They seem to live such painless lives; their bodies are so healthy and strong. They don't have troubles like other people; they are not plagued with problems like everyone else... I get nothing but trouble all day long; every morning brings me pain... So I tried to understand why the wicked prosper. But what a difficult task it is!" (Psalm 73:3–5, 14, 16 NLT).

A word of hope was spoken to the psalmist. God reminded him of the preciousness of a life of faith. "Don't worry about the wicked or envy those who do wrong. For like grass, they soon fade away... For the wicked will be destroyed, but those who trust in the Lord will possess the land" (Psalm 37:1–2a, 9 NLT).

God revealed to David a course of action for the saints to follow in finding contentment in the midst of life's confusion. A five-fold formula, outlined in Psalm 37, is fitting for everyone regardless of the problems endured. "Don't worry (v1); trust in the Lord and do good (v3); take delight in the Lord (v4), commit everything you do to the Lord (v5); be still in the presence of the Lord and wait patiently for him to act" (v7) (NLT).

A person does not enroll in school one day, and then graduate the next day. There is a process to the learning experience: time involved, expectations to develop, goals to achieve, and knowledge to acquire. Life is a school often referred to as "the University of Hard Knocks." Knowledge on living is hard to achieve because life often gives the test first and the lesson later. It is when the ordeals are over that we begin to fully understand the reasons why!

Why do the righteous suffer? As a matter of fact, why does anyone suffer? The overwhelming answer is, "because we are human!" Humanity, in its raw state, is depraved, diseased, damaged, and deplorable! What is the potential outcome of human suffering? Are there any positive truths to be learned from these negative experiences?

There is a positive side to suffering. Good results can be obtained. A spirit of overcoming victory can permeate our hearts even on the darkest of days. Helen Keller once said, "We could never learn to be brave and patient if there were only joys in the world."

One aspect of suffering is to *teach* us. Life can be a strict and harsh teacher, but lessons learned the hard way are not easily forgotten. The agony and inconvenience of suffering directs us to become patient patients! Healing takes time. In our limitations, we realize we cannot perform as usual, so we must learn to adapt, to conform, to share, and to wait. Patience is a treasured but learned characteristic. We are more able to endure if we learn to abide. The psalmist confessed, "Before I was afflicted I went astray... It is good for me that I have been afflicted, that I might learn thy statues" (Psalm 119:67, 71 KJV).

Suffering also teaches us to trust the Lord more completely.

Realizing that God blesses in spite of our circumstances encourages us to follow his Word and fulfill his will for living.

He is the Lord of all living, the Master in control. We must learn that we cannot handle by ourselves all the tedious details of aches and pains. We cannot function properly if controlled by a body that is crying out in need. Yielding to the one who knows us and knows what we need is both comforting and challenging. "For your heavenly father knows that you have need of all these things" (Matthew 6:32 KJV). The psalmist reminds us, "The Lord directs the steps of the godly. He delights in every detail of their lives" (Psalm 37:23 NLT).

Suffering is a great teacher. These lessons of life help us to develop strength and wisdom. "We can rejoice, too, when we run into problems and trials, for we know that they help us develop endurance. And endurance develops strength of character, and character strengthens our confident hope of salvation" (Romans 5:3–4 NLT).

"Soaring"
Alice H. Mortenson

Sometimes God takes away our props
that we might lean on Him,
allows temptations, so we'll grow
and triumph over sin.

Sometimes He takes away our strength
for doing earthly things
to rest our bodies that our souls
may soar on eagle's wings.

Let's not resent it when He says,
"Come ye apart—Be still"
or chafe at disappointments
that are His sovereign will.

Oh, let's not doubt or question "Why?"
with unexplained delays,
but keep on soaring 'neath His wings
with gratitude and praise!

Suffering also serves to *toughen* us. The Apostle Paul had a traumatic confrontation with suffering. He referred to his limitations as a "thorn in the flesh." He was hindered from becoming everything he desired to be for the Lord's kingdom. He prayed earnestly and fervently for God to remove this element. God reminded him that "My grace is all you need. My power works best in weakness" (2 Corinthians 12:9a NLT).

Paul grew stronger in spirit and determination. He rebounded with renewed strength. "I take pleasure in my weaknesses, and in the insults, hardships, persecutions, and troubles that I suffer for Christ. For when I am weak, then I am strong" (2 Corinthians 12:10 NLT). Dale Carnegie once said, "Most of the important things in the world have been accomplished by people who have kept on trying when there seemed to be no hope at all."

Salmon swim upstream to spawn. It is a long and difficult journey struggling against the current. Growing stronger in this journey, they are able to leap across massive waterfalls to their destination. Likewise, the "upstream Christian in a downstream world" develops toughness and is able to endure through the hardships of suffering. Here is a blessed truth: "I can do all things through Christ who strengthens me" (Philippians 4:13 KJV).

Throughout his ministry, Paul grew stronger, tougher, and was greatly encouraged in times of trials and weariness. "When we arrived in Macedonia, there was no rest for us. We faced conflict from every direction, with battles on the outside and fear on the inside. But God, who encourages those who are discouraged, encouraged us..." (2 Corinthians 7:5–6 NLT). C.S. Lewis wrote, "God, who foresaw your tribulation, has specially armed you to go through it, not without pain but without stain."

Trials and suffering, when viewed through the eyes of faith, will cause the sufferer to rely on the presence and power of the Holy Spirit. We then can stand tall and tough in the face of any trouble. In His power to strengthen us, we can "fight the good fight of faith" (1 Timothy 6:12 KJV). We will be capable of facing grief and death knowing "thou art with me" (Psalm 23:4 KJV). We can find assurance when the suffering we are enduring seems to be a discipline from God and rejoice because "thy rod and thy staff they comfort me" (Psalm 23:4b KJV). When in the presence of those who dislike me and would inflict harm upon me, the Spirit gives strength to "pray for those which despitefully use you, and persecute you" (Matthew 5:44 KJV).

Suffering will also *tender us*. The same sun that hardens clay will melt butter. The difficulties of life will either make a person bitter or better! Aches and pains, distresses and discomforts have the capacity to soften our attitudes toward other fellow sufferers. It is the crushed grape that yields the wine. We can better understand their complaint when we share in their condition. We have no right to criticize the sobs and groans of others until we have first "walked a mile in their shoes!" In our suffering, we identify with their heart cries. Jesus, the suffering servant, was moved with compassion toward the crowds when he saw "they were confused and helpless, like sheep without a shepherd" (Matthew 9:36 NLT).

Believers are urged to "be kind one to another, tenderhearted, forgiving one another" (Ephesians 4:32 KJV). Sincere sympathy is a grace greatly appreciated when shared with struggling souls. Sympathy shared is empathy. Sympathy senses a burden; empathy shares the burden. Sympathy realizes the hurts but empathy responds to those hurts. "Bear ye one another's burdens, and so fulfil the law of Christ" (Galatians 6:2 KJV). "Don't just pretend to love others. Really love them... Be happy with those who are happy, and weep with those who weep" (Romans 12:9, 15 NLT). "Brethren, if a man be overtaken in a fault, ye which are spiritual, restore such a one in the spirit of meekness; considering thyself, lest thou also be tempted" (Galatians 6:1 KJV).

The Apostle Paul wrote often of his struggles. In these trials, he was drawn closer to the Lord and more useable as a servant in the kingdom of God. We too will benefit from life's struggles and be blessed when sharing in the struggles of others. "God is our merciful Father and the source of all comfort. He comforts us in all our troubles so that we can comfort others. When they are troubled, we will be able to give them the same comfort God has given us" (2 Corinthians 1:3–4 NLT).

The Celebration of Suffering

"To God Be the Glory!"

TEXT: "Now a certain man was sick, named Lazarus, of Bethany, the town of Mary and her sister Martha… Therefore his sisters sent unto him [Jesus], saying, Lord, behold, he whom you lovest is sick. When Jesus heard that, he said, This sickness is not unto death but for the glory of God that the Son of God might be glorified thereby" (John 11: 1, 3–4 KJV).

In Bethany lived a family who were dear and precious friends with Jesus. Lazarus and Jesus shared many things in common. When he became sick, Mary and Martha sent word to Jesus that his dearest friend needed him to come for a visit. The sisters recognized the bond between them so the message sent to Jesus read, "Lord, behold he whom you lovest is sick" (John 11:3 KJV).

The welcome mat was always out for Jesus to visit. Martha was the "busy bee" in preparing for Him to come. She wanted everything in order, the house to be clean and tidy, meals planned, and the guest room ready for this honored friend. Mary could hardly wait for Jesus to arrive. Her heart was full of love for the Lord. She would sit and listen intently as he talked of the heavenly Father and of the kingdom of heaven.

The explanation Jesus gave Lazarus's illness was confusing to the disciples and to the sisters. At first he said, "This sickness is not unto death but for the glory of God" (v4a). A few days later he declared, "Our friend Lazarus sleepeth; but I go, that I may awake him out of sleep (v11). When the disciples misunderstood this word, he declared, "Lazarus is dead. And I am glad for your sakes that I was not there, to the intent ye may believe; nevertheless let us go unto him" (vs 14–15).

Martha met Jesus with a sharp rebuke, "Lord, if thou hadst been here, my brother had not died" (v21). Even the mourners bewilderedly asked, "Could not this man, which opened the eyes of the blind, have caused that even this man should not have died?" (v37). Mary also expressed a doubtful faith. She also declared, "Lord, if thou hadst only been here, my brother had not died" (v32).

Martha's faith had only a glimmer of hope as she continued "But I know, that even now, whatsoever thou wilt ask of God, God will give it thee" (v22). I have often wondered what she expected Jesus to do at this point in time. Restoring him to life was the only alternative, and this had been the plan of Jesus from the beginning. Oh, what a promise he made to Martha, "Thy brother shall rise again" (v23).

So caught up in traditional beliefs concerning the resurrection, she failed to grasp the truth of Jesus's promise. This she knew: "that he shall rise again in the resurrection at the last day" (v24). It was beyond her reasoning to believe that Jesus could raise Lazarus back to life.

The purpose of Jesus for this restoration to life miracle was two-fold. It was to declare the "glory of God" and to establish a basis for faith that "you may believe." How was God to receive glory? Jesus was to perform a miracle of life that was unparalleled and unknown in medical science and religious beliefs of the day.

Jesus wanted them to believe that he is of the heavenly Father and that He is "the resurrection and the life" (v25). Jesus did not go to Bethany to heal the sick but to raise the dead. Hundreds of people had been healed. This had become an excepted miracle, a familiar work of the Lord. Many were taking advantage of this grace by receiving the miracle but rejecting the Master. They enjoyed the gift, but they failed to give God the glory.

Jesus would now carry them to a new level of faith. To Martha he said, "He that believeth in me, though he were dead, yet shall he live: And whosoever liveth and believeth in me shall never die. Do you believe this?" (v25–26). As they stood at the grave, Jesus reminded her again, "Said I not unto thee, that, if thou wouldest believe, thou shouldest see the glory of God?" (v40).

The raising of Lazarus was truly a glorious miracle. Through this experience we understand that God is to receive glory in our burdens and in his blessings. To give God the glory is to praise him, to laud his might and majesty. In giving God the glory, we recognize that he is the Lord of life and that he rules over all life and death, sickness and health, strengths and weaknesses. He is Lord!

In everything we do, God is to be glorified. Whether therefore you eat, or drink, or whatsoever ye do, do all to the glory of God" (1 Corinthians 10:31 KJV). Since the saved are justified by faith, we "rejoice in hope of the glory of God" (Romans 5:2 KJV). We are to do ministry in a manner that "God in all things may be glorified through Jesus Christ" (1 Peter 4:11b KJV).

With faith in Christ, we will "glory in tribulations" (Romans 5:3 KJV). Through God's grace we will "glory in my [our] infirmities, that the power of Christ may rest upon me [us]" (2 Corinthians 12:9 KJV). In times of great blessings, we shall behold the glory of the Lord. "The wilderness and the solitary place shall be glad for them; and the desert shall rejoice, and blossom as the rose...they shall see the glory of the Lord, and the excellency of our God" (Isaiah 35:1–2 KJV).

Jesus had said to Martha, "If thou wouldest believe, thou shouldest see the glory of God?" (John 11:40). Isaiah prophesied, "Then your salvation will come like the dawn...and the glory of the Lord will protect you" (Isaiah 58:8 NLT).

God desires that we "see his glory in all areas of life." When we understand that God desires to be glorified in our lives regardless of the circumstances, then nothing else matters except "to God be the glory!"

Know that whatever happens to us in this body can bring glory to God. Giving glory to God in all things will bring the greatest peace and rejoicing ever to be experienced. Miracles are awaiting us when we give God the glory. "This sickness is not unto death, but for the glory of God" (John 11:4).

On one occasion, the teachings of Jesus were misunderstood by the trained religious leaders but completely grasped by the simple-minded. Jesus prayed, "O Father, Lord of heaven and earth, because thou hast hid these things from the wise and prudent, and hast revealed them unto babes. Even so, Father: for so it seemed good in thy sight" (Matthew 11:25–26 KJV).

God views his work toward us as good and pleasurable. His will for our lives is rewarding. He rejoices in our faith and faithfulness. We have been adopted into the family of God "according to the good pleasure of his will (Ephesians 1:5 KJV). Men are saved through the preaching of the Word because "it pleased God by the foolishness of preaching to save them that believe" (1 Corinthians 1:21 KJV). The kingdom of God is available to all who believe because "it is your [the] Father's good pleasure to give you the kingdom" (Luke 12:32 KJV).

In the same manner that God said of Jesus, "This is my beloved Son, in whom I am well pleased" (Matthew 3:17 KJV). God is also pleased with his people. "For the Lord taketh pleasure in his people: he will beautify the meek with salvation" (Psalm 149:4 KJV).

Whether we understand it or not, whatever we may face in life is used of God to further his kingdom. Nothing takes God by surprise. He will use both good and bad experiences to bring glory to his name. "For it is God which worketh in you both to will and to do of his good pleasure" (Philippians 2:13 KJV).

A few days following the raising of Lazarus, a banquet was given in Jesus's honor in the home of Mary, Martha, and Lazarus. Many people came not only to see Jesus but to better grasp the reality of such a miracle of life. They came to see Lazarus! The chief priests were enraged and ready to kill Lazarus because of the attention and praise being given Jesus by the Jewish community. Because that by reason of him (Lazarus) many of the Jews went away and believed in Jesus. The Pharisees said among themselves. Behold, the world is gone after him." (John 12:11, 19 KJV) The greatest glory God can receive is for people to believe in his Son as Savior and Lord.

At the grave, Jesus had said to Martha, "Said I not unto thee, that, if thou wouldest believe, thou shouldest see the glory of God?" (John 11:40 KJV). Oh, to see the glory of God! Look around you. God is at work in and through it all! "We know that all things work together for good to them that love God, to them who are the called according to his purpose" (Romans 8:28 KJV).

The Apostle Paul, in his farewell speech, assured the church at Ephesus of his peace in the midst of peril, "And now, behold, I go bound in the spirit unto Jerusalem, not knowing the things that shall befall me there: Save that the Holy Ghost witnesses in every city, saying that bonds and afflictions abide me. But none of these things move me" (Acts 20:2–23a KJV). Paul was not moved by these negative expectations. His hope was in the promises and power of God. The theme of his life seemed to be "In everything give thanks [glorify God]: for this is the will of God in Christ Jesus concerning you" (1 Thessalonians 5:18 KJV).

"The Weaver"
Grant Tullar

My life is but a weaving
Between my God and me.
I cannot choose the colors
He weaveth steadily.

Oft' times He weaveth sorrow;
And I in foolish pride
Forget He sees the upper
And I the underside.

Not 'til the loom is silent
And the shuttles cease to fly
Will God unroll the canvas
And reveal the reasons why.

The dark threads are as needful
In the weaver's skillful hand
As the threads of gold and silver
In the pattern He has planned...

"Our Father, which art in heaven, Hallowed be thy name. Thy kingdom come, Thy will be done in earth, as it is in heaven... For thine is the kingdom, and the power, and the glory, for ever. Amen" (Matthew 6:9–10, 13 KJV).

The Challenge to Survive

"Closed for Repairs!"

"Seventy years are given to us! Some even live to eighty. But even the best years are filled with pain and trouble; soon they disappear, and we fly away" (Psalm 90:10 NLT).

One evening, a friend and I drove to a neighboring city to share a meal at a popular Italian restaurant. On the way, we discussed the menu. We could hardly wait to try their renowned pasta sauce. We arrived early so as to avoid a large crowd. However, the parking lot was totally empty, and a large sign covered the front entrance. The sign read "Closed for Repairs."

The universe is vast and far-reaching, yet God has imposed limitations and restrictions on all areas of creation. "You placed the world on its foundation so it would never be moved. You clothed the earth with floods of water... Then you set a firm boundary for the seas, so they would never again cover the earth" (Psalm 104:5–6, 9 NLT).

Every living creature is distinct and diverse. Each has innate natural limitations that keep order and existence in check. This is especially true for human life and the human body. The violation of these natural limitations give way to hurts of all types.

The Superman Syndrome, where we leap tall buildings in a single bound, causes some people to press beyond reasonable limits.

A person may work long hard hours, complete double shifts week after week, and still try to keep a full schedule of family, community, church, and personal life activities. We try to go it on four hours of sleep each day, pop a handful of multivitamins, gulp down "5-hour" energy drinks, and give the appearance of being normal. Like the Energizer Bunny, we try to keep going and going! Our motto for life seems to be "This is no time to slow down. I have places to go, people to see, and things to do!"

Surviving an exciting ride on the circus carousel can be exhausting. You purchase a ticket, mount your wooden steed, and hold on for the ride of your life. Music plays, lights flash, and the merry-go-round continues to go up and down, around and around, until the ride is finished.

We felt scared but then we settled in to enjoy the ride. All too soon it was over! During the ride, we experienced several different emotions. There was a thrill, then a chill! We laughed and cried. We held on for dear life, then we let go and acted so brave—"Look, Mom, no hands!" At first, we were reluctant to get on; then at long last, we did not want to get off when the whirl of the adventure was over. We were dizzy and wobbly trying to walk away.

The merry-go-round of life is much the same way with its ups and downs and rounds and rounds! There is forward progress, but we never seem to get anywhere. We find ourselves holding on, hoping to last until the ride is over. The crowd becomes a blur passing by so fast! We can't look! We're too dizzy to focus! Our stomachs churn! We break out in a sweat. We feel we're about to fall, to plunge headlong into the waiting crowd. "Stop the world, I want to get off!" But you have to wait until the music stops. "Why, oh why, didn't I just sit on the park bench?"

Those who choose to "sit on the bench and watch the world go by" may never know the thrill of victory. They do, however, share "the agony of defeat." Bench warmers may also become dizzy and dazzled as they watch life move on around them. Their enjoyment is simply the moments of rest afforded by the bench. Their decision to "sit this one out" hides from public view the woes of the pain and problems they face. "I'm tired. I'll just sit here for a while." "My feet hurt." "My ankles are swollen." "My back feels tight." "I am getting a headache from all this noise." "We'd better head home. I think I'm going to be sick!"

Oh, the challenge to keep going, to push the limits, or just to survive! Active or idle, positive or negative, there seems to be no escape from this vicious cycle of being human! These experiences are all a part of living. "My life is full of troubles… I am as good as dead, like a strong man with no strength left" (Psalm 88:3a, 4 NLT). "People are born for trouble as readily as sparks fly up from a fire" (Job 5:7 NLT).

The human body is a remarkable machine, but machines wear out with use. Toys get broken when abused. Expensive jewelry may tarnish when neglected. The human body can also be neglected, abused, pushed to the limits, and broken. Regular nourishment and rest are essential in keeping the body strong and healthy. Periodic breaks from our routines are needed in maintaining a clear mind and a rejuvenated body. As limited beings, we are feeble and frail. Proper care of our body is a must. We need to "Close for Repairs." Today, many are saying, "This is my body. I have the right to make decisions on what I do with and in my body." In reality, these bodies are gifts from God. The very breath of life comes from him. We are responsible and accountable to God for our bodies. A biblical reminder is "know ye not that your body is the temple of the Holy Ghost which is in you, which ye have of God, and you are not your own? For ye are bought with a price: therefore glorify God in your body…" (1 Corinthians 6:19–20).

On a hot July afternoon, while working in the flower garden, a strange sensation came over me. The summer heat was nearing 100 degrees, but I felt cold with a spine-tingling chill. My head began spinning! Everything went dark! My heart was pounding like a bass drum in my head. A piercing pain penetrated my chest. I fell to the ground in the middle of the petunias! A neighbor rushed to my aid and called 911. At the ER everyone was in a rush to revive me—an IV in the arm, CO2 mask on my face, little pill under my tongue, adhesive stickers to the chest, wires connected for EKG, and a heart monitor. The "vampire nurse" drew vials and vials of blood for testing. There were X-rays, a CT scan, and a sponge bath.

Soon the cardiologist was sitting on the side of my bed.

"Well, you missed the big one this time. You may not be so lucky in the future unless you change your stressful ways. Your heart is okay. No blockages, no sign of stroke or heart attack. You were only having 'heart spasms.'"

"Oh, doc," I asked, "what caused a heart spasm? Why and how? What can I do to prevent another one?"

"Stress, my boy, anxiety and exhaustion! You are all tied up in a knot inside. Stressed out! Your nerves are a stick of dynamite lit at both ends and ready to explode!"

The cure he said was up to me.

"You must give it a break! Let some things go!"

The prescription he wrote was simple and easy to follow.

"Take a twenty-minute rest break every day after lunch."

Surely there would be more to it than that—some pills or tonic, portable oxygen, a heart monitor, further testing. No, the doctor reminded me again, all that is needed is "learn to relax and take care of my body."

Though in doubt, I started this daily regimen. After a few days, I could hardly believe the difference in how refreshed I felt. This is a continuing routine, and I find it to be as rewarding to my soul as to my body. God had already prescribed this routine for man. "But they that wait upon the Lord shall renew their strength; they shall mount up with wings as eagles; they shall run, and not be weary; they shall walk, and not faint" (Isaiah 40:31 KJV).

The strain and stress of survival experienced by a young minister in Philippi illustrates this truth. The Apostle Paul's friend—Epaphroditus—literally made himself sick from overwork. "Because for the work of Christ he was nigh unto death, not even regarding his life, to supply your lack of service toward me" (Philippians 2:30 KJV). His motto was "the work must go on regardless!" When the saints at Philippi failed to supply all that was needed for Paul's ministry, this young man got busy. He worked beyond the limits putting his own life in jeopardy. In his eagerness for the church to succeed, he was killing himself for the ministry. He tried to make up for the slack in others. He did so out of his love for Christ and his admiration for the apostle. But one man can only do what one man can do. We are responsible for our labors only. The Lord desires a living sacrifice, not a dead one!

In six days, God completed this vast creation. On the seventh day, God rested. God designed a "Sabbath day" for rest. God even designed a "Sabbath year" and commanded the people of Israel to allow the land to lie fallow for a season. Machinery needs to cool down and be serviced and maintained. The human body is even more delicate and must be allowed time for rest and recovery. Rest breaks from our labor, a vacation or just a day off occasionally are vital and healthy aspects for living. A person can only do what the mind and body can tolerate. If we work beyond the limits, we will pay the consequences. One may tire easily, lose concentration, and experience burnout.

On one occasion, the disciples worked feverishly ministering to the hurting masses. "For there were many coming and going and they had no leisure so much as to eat, and Jesus said, 'Come ye yourselves apart into a desert place, and rest for a while'" (Mark 6:31 KJV).

Jesus offers a wonderful solution for our human dilemma, "Come unto me, all ye that labour and are heavy laden, and I will give you rest" (Matthew 11:28 KJV).

The Consequences of the Curse

"Don't Stop at the ER. Get Me to the Morgue!"

"Joseph died at the age of 110. The Egyptians embalmed him, and his body was placed in a coffin in Egypt" (Genesis 50:26 NLT).

Serious attempts are being made to diagnose the causes for the debilitating depths of human suffering. The prevention of disease is at the heart of modem medical research. Eliminating all suffering for man and beast is a priority with pharmaceutical laboratories, medical clinics, and religious organizations alike. One pharmacy chain directs patients to their stores located at the "Corner of Healthy and Happy!" That is what we desire, to live and laugh, to be healthy and happy, but the curse of being human stands in our way and its consequences are inescapable.

How unusual this text concerning Joseph. The last verse of the book of Genesis, the book of beginnings, the book of life ends with a death and a "coffin in Egypt." The book which begins with "In the beginning, God created" ends with "so Joseph died." Genesis tells how God "formed man of the dust of the ground and breathed into his nostrils the breath of life" and closes with "the Egyptians embalmed Joseph."

Sickness, weakness, disease, and death are all a part of the process of living. Alexander Pope, an English poet of the 1700s, was crippled by illness at the age of twelve. His entire life was a struggle with pain and inconveniences. On his deathbed, the doctor assured him that his breathing was easier, his pulse steadier, and various other encouraging things. "Here I am," commented Pope to a friend, "dying of a hundred good symptoms."

While browsing through the health and wellness section of a bookstore, I was amused by the various titles. One read, *Munch and Crunch: Pack it in and Work it off!* One other title was *Right Eating for Right Living.* The title that really caught my attention was *Eat Right, Work Hard, We Die Anyway.* In the self-help section, I found this amusing title *How to Live to Be 100 or Die Trying.*

The psalmist contemplated his existence with a lament. "I have been sick and close to death since my youth. I stand helpless and desperate…" (Psalm 88:15 NLT). Job also shared his summation of life, "My spirit is crushed, and my life is nearly snuffed out. The grave is ready to receive me" (Job 17:1 NLT).

From the beginning, in the garden, the disobedience of Adam and Eve brought a curse upon all humanity. Adam was created a "living soul." He was given the stipulation forbidding the eating from the tree of the knowledge of good and evil. A stern warning concerning the consequence of this disobedience was stressed. "But of the tree of the knowledge of good and evil, thou shalt not eat of it: for in the day that thou eatest thereof thou shalt surely die [in dying thou shalt die]" (Genesis 2:17 KJV).

What a tragedy! "Wherefore, as by one man sin entered into the world, and death by sin; and so death passed upon all men, for that all have sinned" (Romans 5:12 KJV). "For the wages of sin is death…" (Romans 6:23 KJV). A part of the consequence upon Adam—thus, on all humanity—was a curse of limitation, pain, disappointment, hard work, and finally, physical death. "Unto the woman he [God said]…in sorrow thou shalt bring forth children… and unto Adam he [God] said…cursed is the ground for thy sake; in sorrow shalt thou eat of it all the days of thy life… In the sweat of thy face shalt thou eat bread, till thou return unto the ground; for out of it wast thou taken: for dust thou art, and unto dust shalt thou return" (Genesis 3:16–19 KJV).

In one of the newspaper columns, "Hints from Heloise," a woman had asked the origin of house dust. The reply was "House dust is a formation of dead skin cells!" In our last spring house cleaning, I found about a dozen "dead bodies" hiding under the den sofa! Human body dead skin cells are a simple reminder that our bodies are deteriorating and we are dying.

While hiking in the Great Smokey Mountains National Park, I came to a point where the trail I was following to Grotto Falls was met by an unmarked trail. A sign to the falls pointed to the right. I searched through the undergrowth to find a sign long since worn and damaged by the weather. The sign read, "Baskins Cemetery," and the arrow pointed in the opposite direction of the falls.

My curiosity and imagination began to run wild. The trail was overgrown and barely visible, but I took the challenge. Making my way through tall briars and thick cane, I followed the trail as it meandered through an old growth hemlock forest. A rippling stream flowed nearby. Soon the trail crossed the stream and wound upward around the mountain edge. Eventually, I came to a clearing, the location of the cemetery. There were thirty-six small graves marked only with a sandstone for a marker, no names nor dates. I mused in wonder of the little mountain community that once inhabited this area. How many families were connected to these graves? Why were they all so small? Were they children? Had they died in the cold winter of pneumonia?

I searched the nearby area for clues of this once happy place. There were no signs of homesteads, no reminders of barns nor fields. Everything was missing except for the graves. With pen and pad from my backpack, I jotted down reminders of the day.

When people die, houses deteriorate, fields lay barren, roads and trails soon disappear. All that's left to remind others of our existence are the grave markers.

The aged and sick king David reminded Solomon, "I go the way of all the earth" (1 Kings 2:2 KJV). Joseph nearing his death, encouraged his brothers, "I die: but God will surely visit you" (Genesis 50:24 KJV). The Apostle Paul reminds us "For as in Adam all die" (1 Corinthians 15:22 KJV).

A somber detailed account of life from the cradle to the grave is found in Ecclesiastes 12:1–7. The New Living Translation is a beautiful poetic description of this aging process.

> Don't let the excitement of youth cause you to forget your Creator. Honor him in your youth before you grow old and say, "Life is not pleasant anymore."
>
> Remember him before the light of the sun, moon, and stars is dim to your old eyes and rain clouds continually darken your sky.
>
> Remember him before your legs—the guards of your house—start to tremble; and before your shoulders—the strong men—stoop. Remember him before your teeth—your few remaining servants—stop grinding; and before your eyes—the women looking through the windows—see dimly.
>
> Remember him before the door to life's opportunities is closed and the sound of work fades. Now you rise at the first chirping of the birds, but then all their sounds will grow faint.
>
> Remember him before you become fearful of falling and worry about danger in the streets; before your hair turns white like an almond tree in bloom, and you drag along without energy like a dying grasshopper, and the caperberry no longer inspires sexual desire. Remember him before you near the grave, your everlasting home, when the mourners will weep at your funeral.
>
> Yes, remember your Creator now while you are young, before the silver cord of life snaps and the golden bowl is broken. Don't wait until the water jar is smashed at the spring and the pulley is broken at the well. For then the dust will

return to the earth, and the spirit will return to God who gave it."

Some illnesses are directly attributed to the use and abuse of unhealthy products or of an immoral lifestyle. Smoking tobacco is thought to be the origin of lung cancer. However, many people who have never smoked have been diagnosed with lung cancer.

The most common cause of cirrhosis of the liver is alcohol abuse. But not all who are alcohol-dependent drinkers have cirrhosis.

Not all illnesses are symptoms of a particular sin. Just because you have the flu or break a leg or suffer from diabetes or any of 1,001 other diagnoses is no sign that God is punishing you for sin or wrongdoing. Sickness affects man in all areas and in all ages of life. Sickness is no respecter of persons. Sickness will knock a strong man to his knees, wrap a baby in a blanket of fever and congestion, choke the breath from an elderly man, and stop the heart of an athlete.

The Bible provides a clear illustration that the results of willful disobedience is illness and death. The Apostle Paul confronted the church at Corinth over their blatant desecration of the Lord's Supper observance recorded in 1 Corinthians 11:27–30 NLT.

"So anyone who eats this bread or drinks this cup of the Lord unworthily is guilty of sinning against the body and blood of the Lord. That is why you should examine yourself before eating the bread and drinking the cup. For if you eat the bread and drink the cup without honoring the body of Christ, you are inviting God's judgment upon yourself. That is why many of you are weak and sick and some have even died."

As long as man lives, he will be threatened by this curse. "For we know that the whole creation groaneth and travaileth in pain together...even we ourselves groan within ourselves, waiting for... the redemption of our body" (Romans 8:22–23 KJV).

The ultimate healing of the body is brought about through death. Physical pain and suffering ends, all fears resolved, and all burdens are lifted when death occurs. All the saints of God can shout "Hallelujah!" at this final stage of redemption, for we will then be free from the "curse of being human."

Dame Gladys Cooper, a British actress of the early 1900s, peered into the mirror on the last evening of her life and remarked to her nurse, "If this is what virus pneumonia does to one, I really don't think I shall bother to have it again." She then tottered back to her bed and died peacefully in her sleep.

"And there shall be no more curse…and God shall wipe away all tears from their eyes; and there shall be no more death, neither sorrow, nor crying, neither shall there be any more pain: for the former things are passed away" (Revelation 22:3; 21:4 KJV).

MEDICINES AND MIRACLES

THE BIBLE IS like an ancient medical journal. Dating from the Genesis account of creation throughout eternity in the Revelation, we are exposed to numerous accounts of illnesses and healings.

Miracles are abundant in both the Old and New Testaments.

Many of the prophets displayed miraculous power in healing the sick. Great use of nature's offerings of minerals, herbs, and spices enhanced health and provided healing.

Jesus is affectionately known as the Great Physician. He identified his mission as healing for the soul. "They that are whole need not a physician, but they that are sick… I am not come to call the righteous, but sinners to repentance" (Matthew 9:12–13 KJV).

Jesus healed the sick and restored life to some who had died. He gave his disciples authority to perform the same miracles. The Holy Spirit anointed other believers with the "gift of healing." Life and health are gifts from God.

The following devotions will give us a clearer picture of God's miraculous work in the health and well-being of man.

The Bible

A Record of Physicians and Prescriptions

"My CHILD, PAY attention to what I say. Listen carefully to my words. Don't lose sight of them. Let them penetrate deep into your heart, for they bring life to those who find them, and healing to their whole body" (Proverbs 4:20–22 NLT).

The Bible reads like an ancient medical journal with great emphasis being given to diseases, diagnosis, drugs, and doctors. Beginning in Genesis and concluding in the Revelation are historical accounts of man's struggles with sickness. Agonies and ailments of all descriptions are diagnosed. Medicines and medical procedures are displayed in the care and treatment of patients.

We learn many aspects of the physicians in only a few verses.

For most of the diseases, it was known, that only a miracle from God could bring a cure. Many patients consulted the prophets to seek healing from God.

The physician was thought of by many as a miracle worker equivalent to the prophets with healing powers." And Asa in the thirty and ninth year of his reign was diseased in his feet, until his disease was exceeding great: yet in his disease he sought not to the Lord, but to the physicians" (2 Chronicles 16:12 KJV).

Physicians were often criticized when patients were not healed. Job's three friends were demeaning in their criticism of him in his sickness. He referred to them as "physicians of no value" (Job 13:4 KJV). A woman with a lingering hemorrhage came to Jesus in hopes of merely touching the hem of his garment for healing. Her condition was deplorable after being treated by many physicians. "And a certain woman, which had an issue of blood twelve years, And had suffered many things of many physicians, and had spent all that she had, and was nothing bettered, but rather grew worse" (Mark 5:25–26 KJV).

It was expected that a physician with medicines could bring good health to the people. "Is there no balm in Gilead; is there no physician there? why then is not the health of the daughter of my people recovered?" (Jeremiah 8:22 KJV). Jesus identified the role of the physician. "They that be whole need not a physician, but they that are sick" (Matthew 9:12 KJV).

One physician in the New Testament is honored by the Apostle Paul: "Luke, the beloved physician" (Colossians 4:14 KJV). Paul was afflicted with many health issues. Luke accompanied him on the missionary journeys as personal physician and secretarial aide.

The physicians in ancient Egypt were much like undertakers, scientists, or chemists. "And Joseph commanded his servants the physicians to embalm his father: and the physicians embalmed Israel" (Genesis 50:2 KJV).

The apothecary was an important entity in early biblical times.

The appropriate mixture of oils, spices, and herbs were used for medicinal and embalming purposes. The body of Jesus was anointed with these spices for burial. "Nicodemus...brought a mixture of myrrh and aloes, about an hundred pound weight. Then took they the body of Jesus, and wound it in linen clothes with the spices, as the manner of the Jews is to bury" (John 19:39–40 KJV).

Oils and ointments were often used for aromatic as well as medicinal purposes. A meal honoring Jesus was given in the home of Lazarus. During the evening, Mary "took a pound of ointment of spikenard, very costly, and anointed the feet of Jesus, and wiped his feet with her hair: and the house was filled with the odour of the ointment" (John 12:3 KJV).

In preparing for worship in the tabernacle, Moses mixed spices for a perfume as a "sweet smelling offering" to God. "Take unto thee sweet spices, stacte, and onycha, and galbanum; these sweet spices with pure frankincense… And thou shalt make it a perfume, a confection after the art of the apothecary, tempered together, pure and holy" (Exodus 30:34–35 KJV).

Egyptian apothecaries made great use of natural minerals and spices. Egypt became a popular center for caravan traders. "A company of Ishmeelites came from Gilead with their camels bearing spicery and balm and myrrh, going to carry it down to Egypt" (Genesis 37:25 KJV).

Gilead was an area saturated with these minerals. Spice-producing plants grew in abundance there. The balm or balsam was a medicinal gum. People were instructed to "go up into Gilead, and take balm" (Jeremiah 46:11 KJV). In times of death and great pain, the people were told to "take balm for her pain, if so be she may be healed" (Jeremiah 51:8 KJV).

In the natural creation, God deposited ingredients in the earth which contained healing powers. The children of Israel, on their journey out of Egypt came to a place named Marah where a great need developed. "And when they came to Marah, they could not drink of the waters of Marah, for they were bitter" (Exodus 15:23 KJV). Moses cut down a tree and soaked it in the springs. The result was satisfyingly refreshing.

Elisha added salt to the waters at Jericho which sweetened the water and gave fertility to the land. (*See* 2 Kings 2:19–22 KJV) Elisha was also a skilled pharmacist. When the sons of the prophets were poisoned by wild gourds cooked in a stew, Elisha added meal to the pot as an antidote. The result was "and there was no harm in the pot" (2 Kings 4:41 KJV).

King Hezekiah was greatly ill with a boil. The pain was burning and excruciating and was told that he would die. Isaiah, God's prophet at the time, rendered a remedy. "Let them take a lump of figs, and lay it for a plaister upon the boil, and he shall recover" (Isaiah 38:21 KJV).

The psalmist praised God for natural remedies as "wine to make them glad, olive oil to soothe their skin, and bread to give them strength" (Psalm 104:15 NLT). Wine, as a pain killer, was offered to Jesus on the cross. "They offered him wine drugged with myrrh" (Mark 15:23 KJV). Timothy was advised to "drink no longer water, but use a little wine for thy stomach's sake and thine often infirmities" (1 Timothy 5:23 KJV).

Wine was used to disinfect wounds and often mixed with oil to sooth and heal. When a traveler on the Jericho road was robbed, beaten, and left to die, "a certain Samaritan...went to him, and bound up his wounds, pouring in oil and wine" (Luke 10:33, 34 KJV).

Wine was also recognized as a sedative to sooth emotional problems. "Give strong drink unto him that is ready to perish, and wine unto those that be of heavy hearts" (Proverbs 31:6 KJV).

Modern medications come in many different forms. Some are injections, infusions, ingestions, and inhalers. Medicines may be pills or pads, patches or powders. Some are creams; others are cold packs. There are tablets and tonics, serums and salves, elixirs and emulsions. Some meds are prescribed to "calm you down" while others are to "lift you up." There are meds to ease a pain, while other meds will treat a sprain. Some meds are taken "under the tongue or between the toes, drops in the ears or sprayed up the nose."

Man is still learning today that remedies for many of our ailments are found in nature. The use of spices, herbs, oils, plants, and minerals excreted from these products enhance health and wellness. It was from bread mold that penicillin was discovered. Chemotherapy drugs for certain cancers are made from tree bark.

Throughout eternity, in heaven, there will be no more sickness nor pain nor death. "And God shall wipe away all tears from their eyes; and there shall be no more death, neither sorrow, nor crying, neither shall there be any more pain: for the former things are passed away" (Revelation 21:4 KJV). Growing in heaven is a marvelous and miraculous tree, the tree of life. Its purpose is to provide joy and blessings and to sustain life for all of heaven for all eternity. Of its many flavors and functions, healing is specific. "In the midst of the street of it, and on either side of the river, was there the tree of life, which bare twelve manner of fruits, and yielded her fruit every month: and the leaves of the tree were for the healing of the nations" (Revelation 22:2 KJV).

Not every patient is healed of sickness through a divine miracle. One may be healed through the God-given avenues of modem medicine or the true and tested ancient herbs and spices. However, every patient is under the watch care of the Great Physician. The Lord eagerly waits to bring blessings into our lives. "But when he saw the multitudes, he was moved with compassion on them" (Matthew 9:36 KJV). He is "touched with the feeling of our infirmities" (Hebrews 4:15 KJV).

Anointing a patient with oil combined with prayers of faith were the instructions given to the early church to receive healing miracles. "Is any sick among you? let him call for the elders of the church; and let them pray over him, anointing him with oil in the name of the Lord: And the prayer of faith shall save the sick" (James 5:14–15 KJV).

In the same manner that Jesus, during his earthly ministry, used different techniques in dealing with each patient, He continues to do so today. We must remember not all miracles of healing are physical. God graciously does a work in the heart of man. Often our greatest pains are not in the body but in the soul and the mind.

Notice again that verse: "And the prayer of faith shall save the sick" (James 5:15 KJV). The word does not say "heal" the sick but "save" the sick! A patient may be saved (healed) from depression or guilt or negative living or ugly attitudes or a mean spirit. In the miracles of God, there is restoration and repair and redemption.

Available for Healing

"The Doctor Will See You Now!"

PSALM 103:1–5 "BLESS the Lord, O my soul: and all that is within me, bless his holy name. Bless the Lord, O my soul, and forget not all his benefits: Who forgiveth all thine iniquities; who healeth all thy diseases; Who redeemeth thy life from destruction; who crowneth thee with lovingkindness and tender mercies; Who satisfies thy mouth with good things; so that thy youth is renewed like the eagle's."

The waiting room at the clinic was overcrowded. Luckily for me, I had an 8:30 AM appointment. Patients continued to arrive and sign in at the reception desk, but no one was being called back to see the doctor. The time was already 10:15 AM, and everyone was getting anxious. A nurse stepped into the room and announced, "There has been an emergency at the hospital. Dr. Brown is in surgery and will be delayed momentarily."

A nurse practitioner could honor my appointment but Dr. Brown had been my personal physician for over twenty years. I needed his advice on a pressing issue. I have great confidence in my doctor's word, so I chose to wait. We all rejoiced when the receptionist announced, "The Doctor will see you now!"

Jesus became known as the Great Physician. His miraculous and compassionate healing ministry centered on the greatest needs of mankind. "They that are whole need not a physician; but they that are sick" (Luke 5:31 KJV). He not only saw the disease; he saw the diseased patient.

As a caring physician, Jesus identified man's ailments, and he identified with the ailing man. "But when he saw the multitudes, he was moved with compassion on them" (Matthew 9:36 KJV). The healing ministry of Jesus was all inclusive. No problem was beyond his power.

Jesus relieved patients of their suffering. His healing included forgiveness and cleansing for their sin.

Jesus dealt with demonic spirits that held men as prisoners to psychotic behavior. He cooled fevered brows and calmed fearful hearts. He comforted disturbed minds. He helped the lame to walk and the dumb to talk. He gave sight to blind eyes and insight to blank minds. He caused deaf ears to hear again, and he inspired rebellious hearts to listen. Jesus lifted men from the mire of self-pity and restored dignity to lives once buried in shame. He was truly the Great Physician!

"And Jesus went about...healing all manner of sickness and all manner of disease among the people. And his fame went throughout all Syria: and they brought unto him all sick people that were taken with divers diseases and torments, and those which were possessed with devils, and those which were lunatic, and those that had the palsy; and he healed them" (Matthew 4:23–24 KJV).

Jesus specialized in the diagnosis, treatment, and healing of human patients regardless of age, race, sex, or condition. Like the ole country doctors of time gone by, no appointment was necessary. Jesus provided treatment and healing for the suffering wherever he found them. He cured Peter's mother-in-law of a fever while visiting in their home. A paralytic was lowered through the roof to the crowded room below where Jesus was teaching.

Traveling through the Judean hill country, Jesus met ten lepers and cleansed them. For assurance of their cleansing, they were told to present themselves to the priest in Jerusalem. Bartimaeus, a blind beggar, was sitting by the highway which leads out of Jericho. When Jesus approached him, he cried out for mercy, and the Great Physician gave him sight.

At the pool of Bethesda, many sick people were waiting for a miracle to occur in the water. Jesus singled out only one man in that crowd and asked, "Do you want to be made whole?" Jesus then said, "Take up your bed and walk." Immediately he was healed!

The words of William Hunter's hymn, The Great Physician, captures a picture of the availability of the Miracle Healer.

> The great Physician now is near,
> The Sympathizing Jesus;
> He speaks the drooping heart to cheer,
> Oh, hear the voice of Jesus…

His travels were often interrupted by patients needing healing.

On his way to the home of Jairus to attend the needs of a terminally ill daughter, a large crowd gathered around him in the way. A woman, dying of a prolonged hemorrhage, made her way through the crowd with the hope of "touching the hem of his garment" in order to be healed. Jesus suddenly stopped. Eyeing the crowd, he observed the woman, called her forth, and made her whole (Mark 5:21–34).

The teaching ministry in the synagogue was often delayed because of a plea for help. Once in Capernaum, a man possessed by an evil spirit cried out in protest to Jesus. When Jesus rebuked the evil spirit, the man was released from its power (Mark 1:21–28). Immediately, the popularity of Jesus spread throughout all Galilee.

Jesus was never too busy with other matters not to provide healing and hope to the hurting hearts of humanity. At the close of a long and busy day, people continued to bring the sick to Jesus for healing. "And at even, when the sun did set, they brought unto him all that were diseased, and them that were possessed with devils. And all the city was gathered together at the door. And he healed many…" (Mark 1:32–34a KJV).

The Great Physician used a variety of methods in his approach in healing the sick. He did so for obvious reasons. Foremost in his work was to glorify the Father. "I have glorified thee on the earth. I have finished the work which you gave me to do" (John 17:4 KJV).

He also used techniques in healing, which demonstrated his authority as the Son of God over all diseases, demonic activity, and death. "But that ye may know that the Son of man hath power on earth to forgive sins (he saith to the sick of the palsy,) I say unto thee, Arise, take up thy bed, go thy way into thine house. And immediately he arose, took up the bed, and went forth before them all; insomuch that they were all amazed and glorified God" (Mark 2:10–12 KJV).

Jesus applied methods for healing which demanded faith from all who were involved. "And Jesus said unto him, If thou canst believe, all things are possible to him that believeth. And straightway the father of the child cried out, and said with tears, Lord, I believe; help thou mine unbelief" (Mark 9:23–24 KJV).

The four Gospel writers list thirty-seven different miracles performed by Jesus. Twenty-seven of these are healing miracles! Some miracles were performed in the absence of the patient, merely at the word of Jesus: "Go thy way; thy son liveth" (John 4:50 KJV). Healing was immediate and complete.

To the healing of the blind he gave more extreme direct ion s. He only touched the eyes of two blind men. Another man Jesus took into a private setting and touched his eyes with saliva. To the man born blind, Jesus made a poultice of clay to anoint his eyes. He then commanded him to "go wash in the poo l of Siloam. He went his way therefore, and washed, and came seeing" (John 9:7 KJV).

To a deaf and mute man, the Great Physician placed fingers in the ears and touched his tongue. A leper, Peter's mother-in-law, and others were made whole by the powerful touch from the Master's hand. To hear the message from the precious lips of Jesus, "Thy faith hath made thee whole" were life changing words.

The greatest sickness man suffers is "sin sickness." God often referred to man's sin as a sickness of the soul. "The whole head is sick, and the whole heart faint. From the sole of the foot even unto the head there is no soundness in it; but wounds, and bruises, and putrifying sores…" (Isaiah 1:6 KJV).

Jesus knew his mission on earth was messianic and miraculous. He quoted the prophets to identify this mission. "The spirit of the Lord is upon me, because he hath anointed me to preach the gospel to the poor; he hath sent me to heal the broken hearted, to preach deliverance to the captives, and recovering of sight to the blind, to set at liberty them that are bruised" (Luke 4:18 KJV).

Through the death and resurrection of Jesus, sick souls may receive forgiveness and healing. "But he was wounded for our transgressions, he was bruised for our iniquities: the chastisement of our peace was upon him; and with his stripes we are healed" (Isaiah 53:5 KJV).

For the deep seated disease of man's soul a specialist is needed.

Jesus is that specialist. The Great Physician rebuked demons and restored man to sanity. He raised the dead and restored to life. He repaired brokenness and restored hope for eternity. He relieved pain and restored strength for living. He redeems from sin and restores fellowship with God. "The Lord nurses them when they are sick and restores them to health... Lord, have mercy on me and make me well again..." (Psalm 41:3, 10 NLT).

What a Great Physician! No one was ever rejected. All who asked received. He is sympathetic and caring and is always available. "For we have not an high priest which cannot be touched with the feelings of our infirmities...let us therefore come boldly unto the throne of grace, that we may obtain mercy, and find grace to help in time of need" (Hebrews 4:15a, 16 KJV).

"The Great Physician will see you now!"

Authority vs. Ability for Healing

"AND JESUS CAME and spoke these words unto them saying, All power (authority) is given unto me in heaven and in earth" (Matthew 28:18 KJV).

The performance of miracles is not about power but authority. God is all powerful. Nothing is beyond the power of God. He rules over all. Moses declared, "The Lord shall reign for ever and ever" (Exodus 15:18 KJV).

The psalmist repeats this theme: "The Lord sitteth King for ever" (Psalm 29:10 KJV). "Thy kingdom is an everlasting kingdom, and thy dominion endureth throughout all generations" (Psalm 145:13 KJV). One of the most popular titles for God in the Old Testament is "The Lord of hosts." The faith of the psalmist was solid as he declared "The Lord of hosts is with us…" (Psalm 46:11 KJV).

Jesus is the only begotten Son of God. He too is all-powerful. God has given to him authority over all. "Wherefore God also hath highly exalted him, and given him a name which is above every name: That at the name of Jesus every knee shall bow, of things in heaven, and things in earth, and things under the earth; and that every tongue should confess that Jesus Christ is Lord, to the glory of God the Father" (Philippians 2:9–11 KJV).

The theme of New Testament preaching and the hope of all believers is the authority of the King of kings. "Then cometh the end…when he shall have put down all rule and all authority and power. For he must reign, till he hath put all enemies under his feet" (1 Corinthians 15:24–25 KJV).

Jesus relied on this authority throughout his ministry. As the Creator of all things, Jesus expressed authority over the elements of nature. The first recorded miracle occurred at a wedding in Cana of Galilee. When the supply of wine ran low, Jesus commanded the servants to fill empty pots with water. When they served this liquid to the guests, everyone was elated, expecting the flavor of wine. They were served no ordinary drink. The governor of the wedding feast declared, "You have kept the best wine until now" (John 2:10 KJV). What Jesus does is always better than the very best that man could imagine.

While crossing the Sea of Galilee, a mighty storm arose. Jesus rebuked the wind and waves. Immediately there was calm to the water as well as in the hearts of the fearful sailors. They expressed wonder at his authority. "What manner of man is this, that even the wind and the sea obey him?" (Mark 4:41 KJV).

Jesus, as the Great Physician, demonstrated authority over all harms and hurts man experienced in the body. There was no ill nor illness to man but that Jesus was in control. Leprosy or lunacy, blind eyes or broken hearts, hemorrhages or high fevers, withered hands or lame legs, Jesus healed each one. "As you have given him power over all flesh…" (John 17:2 KJV).

Jesus has authority over something even more serious than man's sicknesses. He can forgive and cleanse from sin. Four very caring individuals brought a paralyzed patient to Jesus. "When Jesus saw their faith, he said unto the sick of the palsy, Son, thy sins be forgiven thee" (Mark 2:5 KJV).

To the woman accused of adultery, Jesus assured her, "Neither do I condemn thee: go, and sin no more" (John 8:11 KJV). The blessed truth of the Gospel declares the authority of Jesus over sin.

"The blood of Jesus Christ his Son cleanseth us from all sin" (1 John 1:7 KJV). "In whom [Christ] we have redemption through his blood, the forgiveness of sins, according to the riches of his grace" (Ephesians 1:7 KJV)

A rabbi is a distinguished and honored Jewish teacher fluent in the language and laws of the Hebrew people. Everyone knew the earthly background of Jesus and his lack of rabbinical training. He was raised in Nazareth and worked in a carpenter's shop, yet he was recognized as the most unique teacher. "And it came to pass, when Jesus had ended these sayings, the people were astonished at his doctrine: For he taught them as one having authority, and not as the scribes" (Mathew 7:28–29 KJV).

Nicodemus was a highly respected ruler among the Jews, a scholar and a teacher. He was convinced that Jesus was the Great Teacher from God. "Rabbi, we know that thou art a teacher come from God: for no man can do these miracles that thou doest, except God be with him" (John 3:2 KJV).

Jesus expressed dominion over demonic spirits. "For with authority and power he commandeth the unclean spirits, and they come out" (Luke 4:36 KJV). In casting out these demonic spirits, Jesus did not hold a séance nor chant Latin phrases. He did not apply a magic potion nor "slay in the spirit" the possessed individual. Jesus commanded the spirits to leave. "Jesus…rebuked the foul spirit, saying unto him, Thou dumb and deaf spirit, I charge thee, come out of him, and enter no more into him" (Mark 9:25 KJV).

The response of the demonic spirits to the command of Jesus was obedience. "And the spirit cried…and came out of him…" (Mark 9:26 KJV). There were times when the spirits worshiped Jesus and begged for mercy.

Jesus ministered with an authoritative word. He doesn't have to perform an act to demonstrate his power. He has "the power" because he has the "authority." He is the one in charge. He is the Lord! "What so ever he saith unto you, do it" (John 2:5 KJV).

Great emphasis is given in the Scriptures to Christ's authority over the power of death. Death is a powerful entity of life. It cannot be avoided. From its grip over the body, we cannot escape. "For as in Adam all die…" (1 Corinthians 15:22 KJV).

Jesus rescued some before death could get the stranglehold. A father came to Jesus with an urgent request. "The nobleman saith unto him, Sir, come down ere my child die. Jesus said unto him, Go thy way; thy son liveth. And the man believed the word that Jesus had spoken unto him, and he went his way. And as he was now going down, his servants met him, and told him, saying, Thy son liveth" (John 4:49–51 KJV).

On three separate occasions, Jesus brought individuals back from the realm of the dead. One was a young girl who had just died. "He went in, and took her by the hand, and the maid arose" (Matthew 9:25 KJV).

A second "rescue from death" occurred as Jesus approached the city of Nain and met the funeral procession of a young man. "And he came and touched the bier... And he said, Young man, I say unto thee, Arise. And he that was dead sat up, and began to speak. Jesus delivered him to his mother" (Luke 7:13–15 KJV).

The third response of Jesus to death was in Bethany at the grave of Lazarus. Arriving in Bethany, he was met by Mary and Martha who grievingly stated, "Lord, if thou hadst been here, my brother had not died" (John 11:21 KJV). Jesus spoke to them the greatest words of assurance concerning life and death. "I am the resurrection and the life: he that believeth in me, though he were dea, d, yet shall he live: And whosoever liveth and believeth in me shall never die" (John 11:25–26 KJV).

At the gravesite, Jesus asked for the stone sealing the entrance of the tomb to be removed. He prayed, "Father, I thank thee that thou hast heard me." In a booming voice Jesus shouted, "Lazarus, come forth." What a wonder of wonders for those who were watching! "And he that was dead came forth, bound hand and foot with graveclothes...and Jesus said, Loose him, and let him go" (John 11:44 KJV).

Two observable theological facts are here noted. In bringing Lazarus back from the realm of the dead, Jesus called out his name with a command, "Lazarus, come forth!" Had he not specified only Lazarus, every tomb in that cemetery would have opened and all the dead would have been raised! "Verily, verily, I say unto you, the hour is coming, and now is, when the dead shall hear the voice of the Son of God: and they that hear shall live... And hath given him authority" (John 5:25, 27 KJV).

A second truth concerns the manner of Lazarus's resurrection.

Lazarus came from the grave bound with grave clothes, linen wrappings much like a mummy. He would wear them again in time to come. This resurrection was more of a rescue mission. Its purpose was to demonstrate Christ's authority over death and to manifest God's glory. "Jesus saith unto her, Said I not unto thee, that, if thou wouldest believe, thou shouldest see the glory of God?" (John 11:40 KJV). When Jesus was resurrected, he left behind his gravelothes folded neatly in place in the tomb. He would never need them again. "I am he that liveth and was dead; and behold, I am alive for evermore. Amen; and have the keys of hell and of death" (Revelation 1:18 KJV).

One final facet in Christ's authority over death is his own death on the cross. "And when Jesus had cried with a loud voice, he said, Father, into thy hands I commend my spirit: And having said thus, he gave up the ghost" (Luke 23:46 KJV). He "gave up the ghost!" Death did not take from him his last breath. Jesus was in control. He presented his spirit to the Father.

Complete authority includes victory over death and the grave. "Christ died for our sins according to the scriptures; and that he was buried, and that he rose again the third day according to the scriptures" (1 Corinthians 15:3–4 KJV). Because he lives, believers can shout "O death, where is thy sting? O grave, where is thy victory… But thanks be to God, which giveth us the victory through our Lord Jesus Christ" (1 Corinthians 15:55, 57 KJV).

Anointed for a Healing Ministry

"'Jesus called his twelve disciples together and gave them authority to cast out evil spirits and to heal every kind of disease and illness" (Matthew 10:1 NLT).

What a motley crew this group that Jesus called disciples. They were the most assorted group of characters one could imagine. At the very beginning, none of them had anything in common with Jesus. The Son of God, a man without sin, whose life was far above average, selected as his cohorts in ministry men who were at the very bottom of society. Some were considered outcasts, renegades, and at least four rugged seafaring men.

One, named Simon, was a crude, cursing fisherman. The other Simon was identified as a Canaanite who had joined a zealot's troop to overthrow the Roman government. Matthew was a tax collector, a hated and despised publican. Along with Simon Peter the fisherman were his brother Andrew and friends James and John, also fishermen. These men were recognized in society as "unlearned and ignorant" (Acts 4:13 KJV). Then there was Judas, a greedy traitor who sold Jesus out for a mere thirty pieces of silver.

Jesus taught these men the things of God. He trained and encouraged them in methods of ministry. He planted the seeds of greatness in their hearts and cultivated them into a harvest of great men. "Ye have not chosen me, but I have chosen you, and ordained you, that you should go and bring forth fruit, and that your fruit should remain: that whatsoever ye shall ask of the Father in my name, he may give it you" (John 15:16 KJV).

Jesus assigned the task of healing and other ministries to these disciples. The miraculous ministry of Jesus was now extended.

Going into all of Galilee, they were to carry on the ministries Jesus had started. "And as you go… Heal the sick, cleanse the lepers, raise the dead, cast out devils…" (Matthew 10:7, 8 KJV).

Did Jesus give to them "power" to perform these miracles? Was this power a special and unique spiritual ability? Were they made into "super disciples" with knowledge and abilities beyond what other believers possessed? Jesus gave them the authority to work wonders.

This authority embodied power associated with the name of Jesus. These disciples could not in their own strength nor in their own name nor with any "say-so" of who they were as disciples work wonders nor signs. However, in the name of Jesus, utilizing authority in his name, miracles were abundant. "And the seventy returned again with joy saying, Lord, even the devils are subject unto us through thy name (Luke 10:17 KJV).

The excitement generated by these miracles was overwhelming.

On one occasion a father brought his demon-possessed son to the disciples. The boy was in a terrible condition. On this occasion, however, the disciples could not complete the miracle. They failed to exorcise the demonic spirit. The father was devastated and reported this to Jesus, "I brought him to thy disciples, and they could not cure him" (Matthew 17:16 KJV). Later the disciples asked Jesus why they were powerless to perform this miracle. The answer revealed a marvelous truth for ministry. "Jesus said unto them, Because of your unbelief…" (Matthew 17:20 KJV).

Miracles of healing are the merciful works of God performed in response to faith. "Is any sick among you? let him call for the elders of the church; and let them pray over him, anointing him with oil in the name of the Lord: and the prayer of faith shall save the sick, and the Lord shall raise him up…" (James 5:14–15 KJV). Bringing the sick to Jesus, either in person or in prayer displays one's faith.

Four men, seeking a miracle, brought their paralyzed friend to Jesus. The crowded building made it impossible for them to reach Jesus. Tearing away part of the roof, they lowered their friend down into the presence of the Lord. These men were faithfully dedicated to this task. They were delighted when Jesus responded with healing. "When Jesus saw their faith, he said unto the sick of the palsy, Son thy sins be forgiven thee... Arise, and take up thy bed, and go thy way into thine house" (Mark 2:5, 11 KJV).

For lack of faith the disciples had failed to cast demons out of a lunatic man. These men witnessed a miracle because of faith. They believed in the authority of Jesus to heal and were determined to carry their friend to Jesus. This miracle was faith in action.

Not only did Jesus extended his authority for ministry, he anointed the disciples with the presence and power of the Holy Spirit to perform ministry. In a resurrection appearance, in the upper room, Jesus anointed them for their special service. "Then said Jesus to them, Peace be unto you: as my Father hath sent me, even so send I you. And when he had said this, he breathed on them, and saith unto them, Receive ye the Holy Ghost." (John 20:21–22 KJV).

Following the day of Pentecost, miracles of healing by the apostles were signs of God's power authenticating the Gospel which they proclaimed. "Many wonders and signs were done by the apostles" (Acts 2:43 KJV). "And by the hands of the apostles were many signs and wonders wrought among the people" (Acts 5:12 KJV).

The response of the people to the disciples because of these "signs and wonders" was phenomenal. "They brought forth the sick into the streets, and laid them on beds and couches, that at the least the shadow of Peter passing by might overshadow some of them. There came also a multitude out of the cities round about unto Jerusalem, bringing sick folks, and them which were vexed with unclean spirits: and they were healed every one" (Acts 5:15–16 KJV).

The first recorded apostolic miracle of healing was performed through Peter and John. On their way to the temple, at the hour of prayer, they encountered a lame man lying near the temple gate. He asked help from Peter and John. Peter's response was "Silver and gold have I none; but such as I have give I thee: In the name of Jesus Christ of Nazareth rise up and walk" (Acts 3:6 KJV). Peter took the man by the hand helping him to his feet. Immediately he received strength and healing. He went running and leaping into the temple worshipping and praising God.

This miracle did not occur by the power of Peter nor in his name as an apostle but in the name of Jesus Christ. The high priest questioned Peter as to the power behind this miracle of healing.

His reply was dramatic: "Be it known unto you all, and to all the people of Israel, that by the name of Jesus Christ of Nazareth... doth this man stand here before you whole" (Acts 4:10 KJV).

In the name of Jesus! Healing took place in the name of Jesus. Demons bowed down and begged for mercy in the name of Jesus. Salvation is available in the name of Jesus. "Wherefore God also hath highly exalted him, and given him a name which is above every name: That at the name of Jesus every knee should bow... And that every tongue should confess that Jesus Christ is Lord, to the glory of God the Father (Philippians 2:9–11 KJV).

Jesus assured all believers of this authority in completing his ministry through the church. "He that believeth on me, the works that I do shall he do also; and greater works than these shall he do; because I go unto my Father" (John 14:12 KJV). In His returning to the Father, the promise of God concerning the Holy Spirit would be accomplished. "It is expedient for you that I go away: for if I go not away, the Comforter will not come unto you; but if I depart, I will send him unto you" (John 16:7 KJV).

The healing ministry of Jesus continued through the work of the Holy Spirit. Jesus urged upon the disciples to know the importance of the Holy Spirit's filling and function in their lives. "And they were all filled with the Holy Ghost... And fear came upon every soul and many wonders and signs were done by the apostles" (Acts 2:4, 43 KJV).

The Holy Spirit actively involved believers in the ministry and mission of the New Testament church. "As they ministered to the Lord, and fasted, the Holy Ghost said, Separate for me Barnabas and Saul for the work whereunto I have called them... So they, being sent forth by the Holy Ghost, departed..." (Acts 13:2, 4 KJV).

The Holy Spirit equips believers to better follow the Lord by giving gifts for service. "A spiritual gift is given to each of us so we can help each other... It is the one and only Spirit who distributes all these gifts. He alone decides which gift each person should have"

(1 Corinthians 12:7, 11 NLT). The Apostle Paul made reference to "those who have the gift of healing" (l Corinthians 12:27 NLT).

The church, the body of believers in Christ, is so spiritually equipped by the Holy Spirit as to meet every need, to furnish every lack, to accomplish every goal, and to complete the ministry of Christ for every believer and to the world.

Jesus assigned authority for believers to take responsibility for ministry, and he anointed believers with the presence and power of the Holy Spirit to accomplish each task. "But ye shall receive power after the Holy Ghost is come upon you: and ye shall be witnesses unto me" (Acts 1:8a KJV).

HINDRANCES AND HANDICAPS TO WELLNESS

IN TRAVELING ACROSS the country, we may encounter many unforeseen hindrances. Traffic jams cause delays. Road repairs may necessitate detours on unfamiliar roads. Impatient drivers who speed and drive recklessly are at risk for accidents. A flat tire on a hot summer day, on a busy thoroughfare, is stressful and dangerous.

Every person may become vulnerable to many stressful life situations. The response one makes to these situations could be a detriment to good health. Responding in socially unacceptable ways could result in havoc or a heart attack. Some persons may express difficulty in coping with problems. These limitations, real or imaginary, hinder health and healing.

Jesus addressed a number of these problems in his teaching. From his words, we learn how important discipline is for healthy daily living. Failure to maintain rational thinking may place a person's health in jeopardy. Spiritual victory or defeat is determined by our attitudes as we fight the battles of life.

Of the many attitudes mentioned in Jesus' teaching, the following are perhaps the most often abused. Physical health and emotional wellness are greatly affected by these emotions.

Anger

"I Was So Mad. I Couldn't See Straight!"

Text: "But I say unto you, That whosoever is angry with his brother without a cause shall be in danger of the judgment" (Matthew 5:22 KJV).

The story is told of an ole farmer and his wife who were engaged in a heated discussion. The wife was doing the discussing while he just sat silently sipping on his morning coffee. She continued her tirade, accusing him of being a lazy, good-for-nothing skinflint. He continued to sit in silence which made her even angrier. She ran out of the room in a huff but returned with a bucket of water which she poured over his head. "Now, what are you going to say about that?" she demanded. His response was slow as he wiped the water from his brow, "Well, after all that thunder and lightning, I should have expected a little shower!"

"Thunder and lightning" are typical descriptions of a person's reactions when angry. In Norse mythology, Thor was the god of thunder and lightning. In times of storms with loud claps of thunder, people would look toward the sky and say, "The gods are angry today!"

Many words identify this heated emotion: wrath, fury, rage, indignation, vexation, upset, irritated, hot, mad, and in a snit. Our Southern idiomatic expressions add flavor to anger's identity:

"Boiling!" "As mad as an ole wet hen!" "I could bite nails!" "I was so mad. I couldn't sleep!" "I was so mad. I couldn't see straight." Expressing anger has been referred to as "letting off steam." The trouble with letting off steam is that it only gets you into more hot water.

Anger is both a constructive and destructive emotion. Anger can motivate a person toward positive actions. Anger can also tear down work-related relationships, devastate a family, or destroy goodwill among neighbors. The philosopher Aristotle taught that "anybody can become angry—that is easy. But to be angry with the right person and to the right degree and at the right time for the right purpose and in the right way—that is not within everybody's power and is not easy." In the text, Jesus indicated that anger is good, but anger unjustified and out of control is damnable.

To be in the company of those who desire to correct injustices and to stand up for right and decency is refreshing. A Christian citizen should never apologize for voicing opinion or conviction or expressing a truth. Anger is constructive when we get upset over issues like abortion, human trafficking, or civil injustice in society. God desires that believers get involved in the lives and living of his creation. Winston Churchill said, "A man is as big as the things that make him angry."

Jesus is a prime example of one expressing "good" anger. On one occasion in the synagogue, a man with a withered hand approached Jesus seeking a miracle. The crowd, mostly hypocritical Pharisees, watched Jesus carefully to monitor his actions. "And they watched him, whether he would heal him on the sabbath day; that they might accuse him" (Mark 3:2 KJV). The lesson he taught concerned life not laws. "Is it lawful to do good on the sabbath days, or to do evil? to save life or to kill? And when he had looked round about on them with anger, being grieved for the hardness of their hearts, he said unto the man, Stretch forth thine hand…and his hand was restored whole as the other" (Mark 3:4–5 KJV).

Jesus was grieved because of their cruelty to the suffering man. Their unconcern made Jesus angry. This is anger from within, out of convictions for righteousness. Robert Browning identified man's true value: "When the fight begins within himself, a man's worth something."

As a destructive force, anger is at the base of a host of psychological, physical, and spiritual problems. Anger may aggravate ulcers, produce headaches, raise blood pressure, or instigate a panic attack. Remember, you don't get ulcers from what you eat but from what's eating you! "He that is soon angry dealeth foolishly" (Proverbs 14:17 KJV). The New Living Translation states, "Short-tempered people do foolish things…"

The elder brother in the parable Jesus told of the prodigal son is a prime example of bad anger. When the younger son returned home after wasting his life in the far country, the father met him with open arms of forgiveness. A party was given in honor of his return with all of his former friends attending. The elder brother was away from home, out in the fields tending the family business. Coming home, he heard music and laughter. He asked a servant as to the meaning of the party. "Thy brother is come; and thy father hath killed the fatted calf, because he has received him safe and sound. And he was angry, and would not go in" (Luke 15:27–28 KJV).

In his anger toward his father, he expressed jealousy toward his brother, accosting him with a tirade of slanderous accusations. He pouted like a spoiled brat in a temper tantrum. "All these years I've slaved for you and never once refused to do a single thing you told me to. And in all that time you never gave me even one young goat for a feast with my friends. Yet when this son of yours comes back after squandering your money on prostitutes, you celebrate by killing the fattened calf!" (Luke 15:29–30 NLT).

Anger is identified as the leading cause of most of life's miseries. Excessive anger contributes to accidents, loss of work time, and financial losses in business. Employees have been fired from their positions because of outbursts of anger. To be quick tempered or to fly off the handle could result in a black eye or a cracked ego. Uncontrolled anger may lead to violence. Anger is one letter short of danger! "Anger is cruel, wrath is like a flood, but jealousy is even more dangerous" (Proverbs 27:4 KJV).

No matter the problem we face, marital conflict or alcoholism, child defiance or nervous conditions, the elimination of hostility is the key factor in the solution. "An angry person starts fights; a hot-tempered person commits all kinds of sin" (Proverbs 29:22 NLT). "A soft answer turns away wrath: but grievous words stir up anger" (Proverbs 15:1 KJV).

Anger is an emotion experienced at various times by everyone. In learning to communicate, a baby may express anger with loud outbursts of crying, kicking, and tears. The message they are sending is "Hey, I need a little help here! The child learns that angry outbursts result in attention from others. People of all ages use anger as a manipulation to accomplish their own desire. A person's anger can be used as a warning: "Watch your step around here. I am still mad at you!"

Loud words with voice inflections and ugly facial contortions exemplify anger manipulation. Professional wrestlers stomp and prance around in the arena blowing and gasping like a raging bull to intimidate their opponents.

Anger may develop from other emotions. When threatened, cheated, abused, or embarrassed, a person is hurt and vulnerable.

They feel a need to defend feelings for personal pride. It becomes easy to be critical of others and hold unjustified conclusions of their actions. When I say, "I was so angry. I could not see straight" I have expressed the truth of my situation. When angry, we may not make wise choices and may come to a conclusion without knowing the facts. We have a distorted perception.

Anger can be expressed in one of two methods. It can be hidden and held inward (*Clam up*). Hidden anger is like a seething pot of water about to boil over. The psalmist expressed his heated emotions. "I said to myself, I will watch what I do and not sin in what I say. I will hold my tongue when the ungodly are around me. But as I stood there in silence—not even speaking of good things—the turmoil within me grew worse. The more I thought about it, the hotter I got, igniting a fire of words" (Psalm 39:1–3 NLT).

Anger can be expressed openly (*Blow up*). "He that is soon angry deals foolishly" (Proverbs 14:17 KJV). In a rage because of Israel's disobedience and idolatry, Moses broke all ten of the commandments at one time! "As soon as he came nigh unto the camp, that he saw the calf, and the dancing: Moses' anger waxed hot, and he cast the tables out of his hands, and brake them…" (Exodus 32:19 KJV).

We are urged to deal with life's aggravations and to properly control attitudes. "'Don't sin by letting anger control you.' Don't let the sun go down while you are still angry, for anger gives a foothold to the devil" (Ephesians 4:26–27 NLT). "Cease from anger, and forsake wrath: fret not thyself in any wise to do evil" (Psalm 37:8 KJV).

"Let all bitterness, and wrath, and anger, and clamor, and evil speaking, be put away from you, with all malice: And be ye kind one to another, tender hearted, forgiving one another, even as God for Christ's sake hath forgiven you" (Ephesians 4:31–32 KJV).

Anger is an attribute of God. There are over six hundred references in the Old Testament concerning anger. "God judgeth the righteous, and God is angry with the wicked every day" (Psalm 7:11 KJV). God's wrath is always justified and consistent with his love and mercy. "The Lord is merciful and gracious, slow to anger, and plenteous in mercy" (Psalm 103:8 KJV). "For his anger endureth but a moment, in his favor is life: weeping may endure for a night, but joy cometh in the morning" (Psalm 30:5 KJV).

Depression

❦

"I Am So Blessed; Why Then Am I So Depressed?"

TEXT: "LORD, HEAR my prayer! Listen to my plea! Don't turn away from me in my time of distress… My heart is sick… I have lost my appetite. Because of my groaning, I am reduced to skin and bones… I lie awake, lonely as a solitary bird on the roof… My tears run down into my drink… My life passes as swiftly as the evening shadows…" (Psalm 102:1–2a, 4–5, 7, 9b, 11 NLT).

The praise singer of the Psalms has changed his tune. He is now crooning the blues. He is in such a sad state. He easily could join the "Sad Sack" quartet from an old TV program wailing out their gloom.

"Gloom, despair, and agony on me / Deep, dark depression, excessive misery. / If it weren' t for bad luck, I'd have no luck at all / Ooh, gloom, despair and agony on me!"

In addition to the psalmist, the Bible identifies other great men of faith wallowing in depression.

Moses had a tremendous job, leading one and a half million people through the wilderness. The children of Israel complained about everything. They had nothing pleasant to share with Moses. At one point, he became so distraught he asked God to take his life. "What did I do to deserve the burden of all these people? I can't carry all these people by myself! The load is far too heavy! If this is how you intend to treat me, just go ahead and kill me. Do me a favor and spare me this misery!" (Numbers 11:11, 14–15 NLT).

Job had enough pain and suffering in life to justify his complaint. Without friends to listen and offer compassion, he complained to the Lord. "I am disgusted with my life. Let me complain freely. My bitter soul must complain" (Job 10:1 NLT).

The prophet Elijah challenged the prophets of Baal. God answered his prayer and sent fire from heaven. His courage was deflated with a threat from Jezebel. Elijah tucked tail and ran!

"Elijah was afraid and fled for his life. He went to Beersheba, a town in Judah, and he left his servant there. Then he went on alone into the wilderness, traveling all day. He sat down under a solitary broom tree and prayed that he might die. 'I have had enough, Lord,' he said. 'Take my life…'" (1 Kings 19:3–4 NLT).

Feelings of depression, being down, and frustrated are common and often complicated. A diagnosis for a deeper level of depression can be made by a doctor or psychiatrist. In these severe cases, medicines, therapy, or hospitalization may be prescribed.

The normal "ins and outs" and "ups and downs" of daily existence force us to survive. We learn to endure these flaws and defects: distress, fears, and discouragements. We become experts in diagnosing our own feelings. I may excuse sadness or a cranky attitude by saying, "I feel depressed today!" We may observe the stressful behavior of another person and acceptingly say, "She's just in another one of her moods!"

Depression doesn't play favorites. Periods of hopeless despair, gloom, or pessimistic attitudes are flaws facing everyone. Both male and female suffer. Religious and agnostics all stumble under a load of difficulties. Depression is not inherited like black hair or blue eyes. It is rather a defect in human growth and development.

The Meinrith-Meyer Clinic identifies depression as feelings of sadness and dejection. A person may develop a pessimistic outlook on life. Mental dullness will cause him not to think clearly neither make reasonable decisions. These dull feelings are often displayed in social withdrawal, loneliness, loss of appetite, sleepless nights, and anxieties. Read again the opening test. These symptoms are all present in the psalmist's complaint.

We are prone to hide our despondent feelings from others. We attempt to disguise our true feelings in erratic behaviors. One may react aggressively or with an impulsive temper outburst. Some people attempt to dull their emotional pains with the use of alcohol or drugs. Being the clown or jokester is an attempt to hide one's sorrow, smiling on the outside but hurting within.

In an attempt to cover our feelings, we deny the true problem, making it difficult to accurately identify depression. Am I angry or just irritated? Am I a failure or just frustrated? Am I tense or terrified? Am I seriously ill or only sentimentally sad? Do I need to be looked after or locked up?

There may be a simple identifiable reason for one's depression. Lack of sleep or being exhausted creates mood swings. Improper diet with the lack of necessary nutrition is a contributing factor.

Under stress, the body fails to function to full capacity. The loss of a loved one in death, fear of living alone, and guilt are dark valleys we must travel through.

Feelings of depression are often seasonal! Holiday problems such as loneliness at Christmas, irritating travel schedules, overspending and overindulgence creates grave problems for many. One may have all that "holiday cheer" without any happiness. "Ho, ho, ho" may become "Woe, woe, woe!"

We tend to color code our feelings. "I'll have a blue Christmas without you." "I am in a black hole and can't get out!" "This is one of those dark gray days!" "There's no silver lining in my cloud!"

Memorial times create difficulty for many people. The anniversary date for a loved one's death, a wedding anniversary remembered by a widow or widower, even one's own birthday may hamper happiness. "Happy Birthday! It's the Big Five O!" The aging process is devastating to a person who is striving for perpetual youthful living.

The basic ingredient for depression is selfishness. An "I" problem develops. Our attention turns inward, the emphasis is on "me!" We only consider how miserable we are rather than how blessed we have become. It becomes difficult to focus on reality. We cannot see "beyond our nose" for a solution to our situation.

Feelings of inadequacy and insecurity develop when one is feeling down. "Nothing ever works out for me!" "Everything is my fault!" "No one likes me anymore!" The psalmist so identified this perception. "Have mercy on me, Lord, for I am in distress... I am scorned by all my enemies and despised by my neighbors—even my friends are afraid to come near me. When they see me on the street, they run the other way" (Psalm 31:9, 11 NLT).

When feeling down and depressed, it takes almost no effort to slip into a pattern of negative thinking. Because of the world situation, political unrest, health pandemics, and views from the news media everyone struggles with negativity. Often all that we hear in conversations is negative. "The world is going down the drain!" "Children are going to the dogs!" "Morality has flown out the window!" God reminds us, "For the despondent, every day brings trouble" (Proverbs 15:15 NLT).

"Anxiety in a person's heart weighs it down, but a good word cheers it up" (Proverbs 12:25 CSB). Anxiety, worry, frustrations, and negative feelings are heavy burdens and pull a person down into despair. "A broken spirit saps a person's strength" (Proverbs 17:22 NLT). Good and encouraging words and positive expressions of faith spark hope and raises a person to a cheerful mood. "A joyful heart makes a face cheerful" (Proverbs 15:13 CSB).

How can I feel blessed when I am so depressed? The answer is in our relationship with the Lord. In Psalm 42, the writer describes a time of spiritual longing for things in life to be better. "My heart is breaking as I remember how it used to be" (v4). Israel was oppressed by the taunts of enemies criticizing their faith. "Day and night I have only tears while my enemies continually taunt me saying, Where is this God of yours?"(v3). He longed to attend worship with others at the house of God. "I thirst for God, the living God. When can I go and stand before Him?" (v2).

It is at that moment he realizes that his hope is not in himself but in God. "Why am I discouraged? Why is my heart so sad? I will put my hope in God! I will praise him again—my Savior and my

God!" (v5) He becomes so uplifted in his love for the Lord that he repeats this testimony twice. (Psalm 42:11; 43:5)

Jeremiah was a faithful prophet of God for over forty years. He labored, preached, loved, and cried for the people without having one convert. At times he wanted to quit, to leave the ministry. Each time he was encouraged by the Word of God. "I said I'll never mention the Lord or speak in his name, but his word burned in my heart like fire in my bones!" (Jeremiah 20:9).

Lamentations is a woeful dirge of sadness. In his sorrows, the author remembered the grace of the Lord. "My strength and my hope is perished… It is of the Lord's mercies that we are not consumed, because his compassions fail not. They are new every morning: great is thy faithfulness" (Lamentations 3:18, 22–23 KJV).

Depression is not all bad. We can "feel depressed" without being depressed. We are sad over disappointment or grieve over a death but that mood need not continue. Troubles that bring sorrow may end in joy. God helps us endure. "Weeping may endure for a night, but joy cometh in the morning" (Psalm 30:5 KJV).

In the Sermon on the Mount, Jesus promised hope. "Blessed are they that mourn: for they shall be comforted" (Matthew 5:4 KJV). The word "comforted" is to be uplifted and encouraged. This comfort is not promised to those who are laughing but to those who are languishing in despair. Hope is not offered to those who are surviving but to those who are struggling. When we feel down, God will lift us up. "Casting all your care upon him; for he cares for you" (1 Peter 5:7 KJV).

Fear

"Living in Panic Mode!"

TEXT: "FEAR YE not therefore, ye are of more value than many sparrows" (Matthew 10:31 KJV).

The graveled road passing our house was muddy when it rained but dusty and hard during dry spells. One mile from our house was town. I walked it several times as a boy. Its hills and curves were so familiar I could almost walk it with my eyes closed. There were no street lights and only one house had a security light in the yard. At night, walking this mile was a challenge and to a twelve-year-old boy. It was frightening.

One night, my brother was to bring me home following the movie at the theater. He was late. I had been left in town, so I began the walk toward home. It was late, pass ten o'clock. I was tired and sleepy, but when the last beam from the street light faded behind me, I assure you, I was wide awake!

Surely this was the darkest night of the year! In the shadows, I struggled just to see the road beneath my feet. The wind rustling in the trees sounded of footsteps in the loose rocks behind me. Every noise from a distance grew louder as I trudged on.

I could hear the angry howl of Mr. Jim's ole coonhound. He was vicious and mean. Mr. Jim kept him in a pen during the day, but he was loose at night to stand guard. I was to pass by his house. He would be waiting for me. I swallowed hard and hurried on!

The road ahead circled near a creek by a pasture where cows bedded down for the night. In the fog, their silhouettes appeared as giant turtles slowly moving toward the water. The fence posts lining the pasture stood like tombstones in a forgotten graveyard. This night was so eerie!

By this time my heart was pounding so hard I could hardly breathe. I began to run as fast as my legs would go. Reaching the house, I fell on the steps in a panic and cried. I felt dad's strong hand on my shoulder.

"Son, what's wrong?"

All I could say was "I was so afraid!"

Later, I wondered why I was so afraid. Was it the shadows, a barking dog, or strange noises? These things could never hurt me, but I panicked and lost control. I experienced the incredible emotion of fear for the first time in my young life. Franklin D. Roosevelt spoke of man's greatest fear: "The only thing we have to fear is fear itself."

Fear is an emotion prevalent among people of all ages. It is a response to a variety of real or imaginary situations. Phobias have been diagnosed into numerous classifications. The fear of spiders, of the dark, of failure, of the future, of monsters and mysteries, and many other phobias emotionally paralyzing masses of individuals.

Anticipated fears, worrying over what might happen, or what could have been hinders successful living in the present. "For the thing which I greatly feared is come upon me, and that which I was afraid of is come unto me" (Job 3:25 KJV).

The entire world lives in a panic mode. We are plagued with prejudice, for we are afraid of people who are different from us. We live in suspicion of people of other races or religions.

As children we were afraid of the "monsters" lurking under our beds or in our dreams. Today, much of the world lives in fear of more cruel monsters. Militant extremists are a threat to the world. Religious persecution abounds worldwide. Houses of worship are vandalized. Government embassies are bombed. Sporting events are often targeted. Children are harmed as daycare facilities have been destroyed. Savage gunmen massacre students and teachers in classrooms. Mob violence with rioting in the streets headlines the news. No one feels safe anywhere anymore. We live in a panic mode! Jesus described this panic as he talked of the end times: "Men's hearts failing them for fear, and for looking after those things which are coming on the earth…" (Luke 21:26 KJV).

The first emotional response recorded in the Bible is fear. Adam and Eve disobeyed God's direct command. When God approached them, they ran and hid. "And they heard the voice of the Lord…and Adam and his wife hid themselves from the presence of the Lord… And the Lord God called unto Adam, and said unto him, Where art thou? And he said, I heard thy voice in the garden, and I was afraid" (Genesis 3:8–10 KJV).

Moses' first encounter with God was at the burning bush. God spoke to Moses out of the bush: "…and Moses hid his face; for he was afraid to look upon God" (Exodus 3:6 KJV).

The psalmist trusted the Lord through all of life's frightening experiences.

"He that dwelleth in the secret place of the most High shall abide under the shadow of the Almighty… Thou shalt not be afraid for the terror by night; nor for the arrow that flieth by day; Nor for the pestilence that walketh in darkness; nor for the destruction that wasteth at noonday" (Psalm 91:1, 5–6, 10 KJV).

After Moses died, Joshua was reluctant to lead Israel. God encouraged him to "Be strong and of a good courage; be not afraid, neither be thou dismayed: for the Lord thy God is with thee withersoever thou goest" (Joshua 1:9 KJV).

During the night, attempting to cross the Sea of Galilee, the disciples encountered a raging storm. All attempts to steady the stem through the turbulent waves were futile. The disciples now in panic mode cried out to Jesus for help. "He arose, and rebuked the wind, and said unto the sea, Peace, be still. And the wind ceased, and there was a great calm. And he said unto them, Why are ye so fearful? how is it that ye have no faith?" (Mark 4:39–40 KJV).

With news of the resurrection of Jesus, the disciples returned to the upper room. I would like to believe they were planning for a worldwide evangelistic ministry, but this is far from the truth. They were hiding, shrinking back in fear for their lives. Once again, Jesus came to their rescue, bringing peace to troubled, frightened men. "Then the same day at evening, being the first day of the week, when the doors were shut where the disciples were assembled for fear of the Jews, came Jesus and stood in the midst, and saith unto them, Peace be unto you" (John 20:19 KJV).

"Peace be unto you!" What a comforting word for troubled souls. Peace is the overall result of the ministry of Jesus. Prophecy identifies him as "the Prince of Peace" (Isaiah 9:6 KJV). His sacrificial death on Calvary assures believers of peace with God. "The chastisement of our peace was upon him; and with his stripes we are healed" (Isaiah 53:5c KJV). Not only does he bring peace to troubled souls, "he is our peace!" (Ephesians 2:14 KJV).

Much of Christ's teachings were to dispel man's fear. He taught us not to fear the vengeance of man. "Fear not them which kill the body, but are not able to kill the soul: but rather fear him which is able to destroy both soul and body in hell" (Matthew 10:28 KJV).

Jesus is life. He is the giver and protector of life; therefore, we should not fear. "Fear not; I am the first and the last: I am he that liveth, and was dead; and, behold, I am alive forever more, Amen; and have the keys of hell and of death" (Revelation 1: 17b–18).

On the night of his birth, angels assured the shepherds of peace on earth. And there were in the same country shepherds abiding in the field...the angel of the Lord came upon them, and the glory of the Lord shone round about them: and they were sore afraid. And the angel said unto them, Fear not" (Luke 2:8–10 KJV).

"Fear not" became the headline message for his ministry. A woman with a hemorrhage for many years approached Jesus in the midst of a crowd. She reached out to touch the hem of his garment and immediately she was healed. Jesus assured her, "Daughter, thy faith hath made thee whole; go in peace" (Mark 5:34 KJV).

In the midst of a storm at sea, Jesus walked on the water to rescue the disciples. When they saw him, they were frightened. Jesus spoke a word to calm their fears. "Be of good cheer; it is I; be not afraid" (Mathew 14:27 KJV).

The promise of Jesus has given assurance to souls in all generations. "These things I have spoken unto you, that in me ye might have peace. In the world ye shall have tribulation: but be of good cheer; I have overcome the world" (John 16:33 KJV).

Unavoidable will be troubles and burdens. We will endure heartaches and sicknesses. Fears and worries will always lie in our pathway. These are worldly attempts to tear down our faith and destroy our hope. God equips us with the assets needed for victory. "For God hath not given us the spirit of fear; but of power, and of love, and of a sound mind" (2 Timothy 1:7 KJV).

God's Word provides the answer for victory. Two extremely important verses display the key for successful coping with fear. The first is protection against fear. "What time I am afraid, I will trust in thee" (Psalm 56:3 KJV). Some fears hold a tight grip on life. They cannot be avoided. We will at times be afraid, and in these times, we must trust the Lord.

The second is prevention against fear. "'I will trust, and not be afraid: for the Lord JEHOVAH is my strength" (Isaiah 12:2 KJV). We have this assurance of help and hope in the promises of God.

"Fear thou not; for I am with thee: be not dismayed; for I am thy God: I will strengthen thee; yea, I will help thee; yea, I will uphold thee with the right hand of my righteousness" (Isaiah 41:10 KJV).

Faith responds to fear with praise to God. "God is our refuge and strength, a very present help in trouble. Therefore we will not fear" (Psalm 46:1–2a KJV).

Immorality

"Do You Want Everything You See?"

Text: "Blessed are the pure in heart: for they shall see God" (Matthew 5:8 KJV).

Growing up in a rural area, the highlight of each day was running to meet the postman to receive our mail. The person delivering our mail drove a 1927 Ford A model automobile. My brother and I sat eagerly waiting each day for him to come chugging down the gravel road leading to our house. On the days when he did not stop, we were so disappointed. We were especially excited when he would deliver the new edition of the Sears Christmas catalogue. That catalogue kept us occupied and content until Christmas Day.

By the week of Christmas, many of the pages of the catalogue were worn and torn from overuse. Mom told us to mark those items that we really liked. So with a red pencil, I began to look and wish and mark. One evening, Mom sat down with us and the catalogue and said, "Okay, boys! It's time to decide. Show me what you would like to receive for Christmas."

I began at the front of that wish book and flipped through the toy section page by page. Excitedly, I said, "I want this and this and that and one of those...!"

Sternly Mom took the catalogue out of my hands and declared, "Wait just a minute, young man! Do you want everything you see?"

Strangely enough the truth in these words echo the message of Jesus from the Sermon on the Mount. His teachings give a deeper meaning to the Ten Commandments. "Ye have heard that it was said by them of old time, Thou shalt not commit adultery: but I say unto you, That whosoever looketh on a woman to lust after her hath committed adultery with her already in his heart" (Matthew 5:27–28 KJV).

Lustful eyes are directed by a wanton heart. "Out of the heart proceed evil thoughts, murders, adulteries, fornications... These are the things which defile a man" (Matthew 15: 1 9–20a KJV). "The heart is deceitful above all things, and desperately wicked" (Jeremiah 17:9 KJV).

"Do you want everything you see?" Every individual is guilty of "wanting and looking." "But every man is tempted, when he is drawn away of his own lust, and enticed" (James 1:14 KJV). To be drawn away is to be captivated and controlled by obsessive desires from the heart (mind).

Since compulsive desires can emanate destruction into daily life, God has instructed each generation toward a life of purity. "Who shall ascend into the hill of the Lord? or who shall stand in his holy place? He that hath clean hands, and a pure heart" (Psalm 24:3–4 KJV).

"Blessed are the pure in heart: for they shall see God" (Matthew 5:8 KJV).

"Now the end of the commandment is charity out of a pure heart..." (1 Timothy 1:5 KJV).

"Love one another with a pure heart fervently" (1 Peter 1:22 KJV).

King David's roving eyes set in motion a roller-coaster of heartache and woe. He saw a beautiful woman and lusted for an encounter with her. He disregarded the fact that he was the king, a man after the heart of God and that he was married. This type of relationship is adultery and is condemned by God. What he saw, he wanted.

"David tarried still at Jerusalem. And it came to pass in an eveningtide, that David arose from off his bed, and walked upon the roof of the king's house: and from the roof he saw a woman washing herself; and the woman was very beautiful to look upon… David sent messengers, and took her; and she came in unto him, and he lay with her" (2 Samuel 11:1a–2, 4 KJV).

Job prayed concerning lustful looks: "I made a covenant with mine eyes; why then should I think upon a maid" (Job 31:1 KJV). The beloved disciple writes in the Epistle, "For all that is in the world, the lust of the flesh, and the lust of the eyes, and the pride of life, is not of the Father, but of the world" (1 John 2:16 KJV). The lusts of the flesh and of the eyes are strong desires for that which is forbidden and inappropriate for moral behavior.

The consequences of a lustful life are detrimental to good health. Certain particular ailments are associated with lust: guilt and feelings of despair from unsatisfied longings, ulcers and high blood pressure from worry, frustration and fears from excessive spending, fatigue from burning the candle at both ends to satisfy an abundant lifestyle.

Why is lust considered as a deterrent to good health? "Wanting everything I see" is an extremely selfish attitude. The natural tendency of the heart is selfishness. Man has an ego problem. We want to be the "master of our fate, the captain of our soul." We want what pleases us even when it may not be the right thing to do nor the right thing for us. Consequences of our lust can be harsh and may do harm to self or to others. Lust is strong!

Samson fell prey to this flaw. "And Samson went down to Timnath and saw a woman…and he came up, and told his father and his mother… I have seen a woman… Get her for me; for she pleaseth me well" (Judges 14:1–2, 3b KJV). The end result of this relationship was a broken vow to God, the loss of power and respect, punishment as a slave, and a horrible death to Samson.

God says, "Thou shalt not" but man seems determined to do it anyway.

"And the Lord God commanded the man, saying, Of every tree of the garden thou mayest freely eat: But of the tree of the knowledge of good and evil, thou shalt not eat of it… And when the woman saw that the tree was good for food, and that it was pleasant to the eyes, and a tree to be desired to make one wise, she took of the fruit thereof, and did eat, and gave also unto her husband with her; and he did eat" (Genesis 2:16–17; 3:6 KJV).

Frank Sinatra made classic a song which declares, "I did it my way!" My way is not always right nor is it the best avenue to travel. In going headstrong to have my way, I may lose friends, hurt other people's feelings, neglect my family and responsibilities assigned to me. "Wanting everything I see" has many pains and pitfalls! "There is a way which seemeth right unto a man, but the end thereof are the ways of death" (Proverbs 14:12 KJV).

"Wanting everything I see" is a mark of immaturity. Children and youth are curious creatures. A major part of the growth process is learning our physical features and functions. In adolescence, teens encounter pimples, peer pressures, pornography, physical changes, and parental struggles. Sex hormones develop, and teens often make irrational decisions without understanding the disastrous consequences.

With the popularity and prominence of pornography, sex is displayed in an irresponsible and erroneous manner. Social media places into the hands of innocent children and teens pictures, videos, and information once referred to as "smut, dirty magazines, taboo sex, and XXX movies." These glorify hard core immorality and create mental images which impair relationships.

Many people never escape this warped presentation of sex.

Marriages often fail because of immoral demands from a spouse. Pampering the appetites of the flesh encourages immature and demeaning activities. How sad when an innocent youth in later life becomes a perverted "dirty ole man!"

The Apostle Paul urged young Timothy to "flee also youthful lusts" (2 Timothy 2:22a KJV). "Let no man despise thy youth; but be thou an example of the believers...in purity" (1 Timothy 4:12 KJV). Young women are instructed to be "discreet and chaste" (wise and pure) (Titus 2:5 KJV). Older people are encouraged to "be in behavior as becometh holiness" (Titus 2:3 KJV).

Thinking pure and decent thoughts is a prevention to immoral behavior. "Fix your thoughts on what is true, and honorable, and right, and pure, and lovely, and admirable. Think about things that are excellent and worthy of praise" (Philippians 4:8 NLT).

One must not throw innocence and purity to the wind. As believers, we must exercise discipline in thought and behavior.

"Put ye on the Lord Jesus Christ, and make not provision for the flesh, to fulfill the lusts thereof" (Romans 13:14 KJV).

"So put to death the sinful, earthly things lurking within you. Have nothing to do with sexual immorality, impurity, lust and evil desires" (Colossians 3:5a NLT).

"Abstain from fleshly lusts, which war against the soul" (1 Peter 2:11 KJV).

"They that are Christ's have crucified the flesh with the affections and lusts" (Galatians 5:24 KJV).

After confessing and repenting of his sins, King David prayed a beautiful prayer. May this prayer become the motto by which we live.

"Create in me a clean heart, O God; and renew a right spirit within me" (Psalm 51:10 KJV).

Surviving and Thriving

We have examined sickness and suffering as they relate to a happy and healthy life. We have considered their cause and contemplated their cure. Now let's go a step further. What should be our response to pains and problems? Should we allow the intrusion of these physical and emotional complications to rule our lives? Will we succumb to their debilitating demands? I think not!

Life is for living regardless of our age or station in life. We can either endure or enjoy the burdens and blessings of life. Whether we survive or succeed is a matter of attitude and commitment.

These last devotions are designed for encouragements in living life to the fullest regardless of situations or circumstances. What is your dream for success and happiness in this journey of life? What are your goals, and how do you plan to achieve happiness? Pause in your journey and reflect on where you have been and where you are now. What will be the outcome of your daily existence?

Are you moaning your lot in life and wearily trudging ahead?

Now is the time to be a thoroughbred charging ahead at full speed! You have made it this far in life: you are alive; now survive.

Living Daily

Text: "And Achish said, Whither have ye made a road to day? And David said, Against the south of Judah, and against the south of the Jerahmeelites, and against the south of the Kenites" (1 Samuel 27:10).

These were dark days for the people of Israel. Saul had been chosen as the new king for the people. He exhibited signs of emotional instability often giving way to fits of anger and hostility.

David had been brought into the king's court as a musician and confidant. The music seemed to console the king during these times of mania and panic. On several occasions Saul, in fits of rage, made attempts on David's life so that he was forced to leave the territory for safety. "And David said in his heart, I shall now perish one day by the hand of Saul: there is nothing better for me than that I should speedily escape into the land of the Philistines; and Saul shall despair of me" (1 Samuel 27:1 KJV).

David became a rebel and gathered around him an army of six hundred men. They hired themselves out as "guardian protectors" to smaller cities. As time passed, they became a marauding troop, invading enemy cities creating fear and havoc for everyone in their path.

In the text, David, his troops, and their families joined with the Philistines, longtime enemies to Israel. For a time, they fought in battles alongside the Philistine soldiers. Then they began making raids as allies to Achish, king of the Philistines.

David made regular reports to the king of their activities and accomplishments. The king was delighted with the daily warfare of such a victorious warrior. Achish, eager to know of David's progress, asked an intriguing question, "Where have you made a road today?" This question was ripe with anticipation to know which direction David had traveled, what enemy camps had been destroyed, and what treasures had he plundered. A timely report of the day's travel was demanded from David.

This question is posed to each of us: "What road have you traveled today?" At the end of the day, contemplating its hours and opportunities, did I work or did I waste, did I progress or procrastinate, did I finish or did I fail? How did I live today?

Living daily is *temporary living*. The psalmist, concerned with the brevity and fast-paced of life compared his days to "grass which groweth up. In the morning it flourisheth, and groweth up; in the evening it is cut down, and withereth" (Psalm 90:5b–6 KJV). At the close of a day, sometimes we ask "Where has this day gone? Where did I make a road today?"

Since we are not promised any certain number of days for our life, we must be concerned with fulfilling the days that we live. "Whereas ye know not what shall be on the morrow. For what is your life? It is even a vapour, that appeareth for a little time, and then vanisheth away. For that ye ought to say, If the Lord will, we shall live, and do this, or that" (James 4:14–15 KJV).

The words introducing the theme of a television soap opera were: "As sands through an hourglass, so are the days of our lives." The psalmist painted a picture of daily life: "we spend our years as a tale that is told" (Psalm 90:9b KJV). Children's story books begin with "Once upon a time" and ended with "they lived happily ever after." Life is a story, your own biography!

Each day is a gift from God that's why we call it the present! We must use this "gift of time" to the fullest, for today is our only opportunity. In a philosophy class on one college campus, the teacher wrote on the board this statement: "Today is the first day of the rest of your life!" Then he asked, "Is this statement true or false?" One student responded, "Sir, this is false. Today *is* the rest of our life!"

Life is designed to be a success-motivated existence. In the creation, God implanted into each element of existence the ability to be productive and useful. "And God said, Let the earth bring forth grass, the herb yielding seed, and the fruit tree yielding fruit after his kind, whose seed is in itself" (Genesis 1:11 KJV). "And the Lord God took the man, and put him into the garden of Eden to dress it and to keep it" (Genesis 2:15 KJV).

Jesus identified his own work ethic: "I must work the works of him that sent me, while it is day: the night cometh, when no man can work" (John 9:4 KJV).

"Plant your seed in the morning and keep busy all afternoon, for you don't know if profit will come from one activity or another—or maybe both" (Ecclesiastes 11:6 NLT). Notice the words "keep busy." This is the secret to success and happiness. Idle hands and idle minds may result in impatience and boredom.

"Whatsoever thy hand findeth to do, do it with thy might..." (Ecclesiastes 9:10a KJV). "Yesterday is a cancelled check; tomorrow is a promissory note; today is ready cash—spend it wisely" (Earl Wilson).

"A Bag of Tools"
R. Lee Sharpe

Isn't it strange that princes and kings,
and clowns that caper in sawdust rings,
and common people, like you and me,
are builders of eternity?

Each is given a list of rules;
a shapeless mass; a bag of tools.
And each must fashion, ere life is flown,
A stumbling block, or a Stepping-Stone."

Living daily is *traumatic* living. In life, we must endure many burdens, heartaches, worries, illnesses, disappointments, and fears. We also will enjoy delightful victories, successes, and blessings. Some days the sun shines; other days, clouds and storms prevail. "People can never predict when hard times might come.

Like fish in a net or birds in a trap, people are caught by sudden tragedy" (Ecclesiastes 9:12 NLT).

Time is unpredictable. The words of Jesus are both warnings and inspirations: "So don't worry about tomorrow, for tomorrow will bring its own worries. Today's trouble is enough for today" (Matthew 6:34 NLT).

For many, daily living is survival mode existence. These are people attempting to live in three time zones at once: yesterday, today, and tomorrow! They are knee-deep in the mire of yesterday's problems and become frustrated in trying to "catch up." They keep running around in circles attempting to get ahead of tomorrow's workload. Many of these people are drowning in the midst of today's floods, frantically trying to find themselves and to maintain a sense of reality. A dear ole pastor friend often quoted a quaint expression to describe this dilemma: "The hurrier I go, the behinder I get" (Lewis Carroll).

Where have you made a road today? How important is today? "This is the day which the Lord hath made; we will rejoice and be glad in it" (Psalm 118:24 KJV).

"You must warn each other every day, while it is still 'today'..." (Hebrews 3:13 NLT).

"Consecrate yourselves today to the Lord...that He may bestow upon you a blessing this day" (Exodus 32:29 KJV).

"Ticktock!"
Ralph Culp

The Grandfather Clock is old and worn,
But it was keeping time before you were born!
The secret behind its keeping time
Is to give its mainspring a daily wind!
What we can learn from this ole clock
Is to keep in time with the tick and the tock!
Now here's a word that we know is true—
Live each day as it comes to you!

Living daily is *terrific* living. Each morning we face new challenges and new opportunities. Unique experiences are waiting for us to mount up with wings like eagles and fly away! Each day we live a surprise mode existence.

A thoughtful husband was to prepare breakfast in bed for his wife on her birthday. As he began the preparations he asked, "Honey, what would you like for breakfast this morning?"

She thought for a moment then replied, "Oh, just surprise me!"

Life is filled with surprises. Unexpected blessings from God abound everywhere. "Blessed be the Lord, who daily loadeth us with benefits…" (Psalm 68:19 KJV). "Praise the Lord…who alone does such wonderful things" (Psalm 72:18 NLT). "The faithful love of the Lord never ends! His mercies never cease…his mercies begin afresh each morning" (Lamentations 3:22–23 NLT).

Life holds many surprises from people living around us. A thoughtful gesture from friends is more valuable than finding a buried treasure. A kind word in times of grief, an encouraging compliment when you feel insecure, or time shared when one is lonely is not only thoughtful but precious. "A word fitly spoken is like apples of gold in pictures of silver" (Proverbs 25:11 KJV).

When God called Abraham to leave his home in Ur, he made a promise. "And I will…bless thee…and thou shalt be a blessing" (Genesis 12:2 KJV). What an inspiring thought this is for *living daily*…being blessed and being a blessing!

"Make me a channel of blessing today, / Make me a channel of blessing, I pray; / My life possessing, my service blessing, / Make me a channel of blessing today" (Words and music by Harper G. Smyth).

Daily Living

Text: "This is the day which the Lord hath made; we will rejoice and be glad in it" (Psalm 118:24 KJV).

There is a difference between living daily and daily living!

Living daily emphasizes time calculated on a day-to-day basis. It promotes living each day and utilizing rather than wasting precious hours. Living daily is to promote each day as if it were our last day. In this frame of mind, we take advantage of every opportunity to serve, to grow, to learn, and to love. *We will* press to the max to complete daily assignments and function in a competitive society! Like the Apostle Paul, we "press toward the mark for the prize of the high calling…" (Philippians 3:14 KJV).

Daily living entails the complications of and the commodities needed for human existence. What will we need each day to function and to succeed? The law of supply and demand dictates many decisions. Health and wealth play a major role in the completion of daily plans. Worship and wisdom are essential in directing our paths for daily living.

What is needed for daily living? Ample *supplies* are of utmost importance and are on top of our survival lists. Food, clothing, and shelter are basic ingredients for normal existence. The expenses for rent or a home mortgage, utilities, groceries, and clothing make up the largest part of a family's budget.

These budget items are always on our mind. A growing teenage student comes home from school, raids the refrigerator, and asks, "Hey, Mom, what's for dinner?"

Mom stands looking through the closet, hoping to find a wardrobe appropriate for her new job and sighs, "I don't have anything to wear that looks right!"

Dad sits up late at night pouring over the recent bills, trying to work each item into the budget. That worried look on his face says to the family, "We must become more conservative in spending."

These essentials are so pressing on our hearts until Jesus addressed their importance in the Sermon on the Mount. "So don't worry about these things, saying, 'What will we eat? What will we drink? What will we wear?' These things dominate the thoughts of unbelievers, but your heavenly Father already knows all your needs. He will certainly care for you. Why do you have so little faith?" (Matthew 6:31–32, 30 NLT).

God is concerned about these "vitals for our survival." In the model prayer, Jesus taught us to pray "Give us this day our daily bread" (Matthew 6:11 KJV). Jesus stressed both the period and the product by saying, "this day our daily bread."

In the wilderness, God fed the children of Israel with manna (bread) from heaven. "Behold, I will rain bread from heaven for you; and the people shall go out and gather a certain rate every day… they gathered it every morning, every man according to his eating" (Exodus 16:4, 21 KJV).

Just as Jesus taught us to have faith in God to supply our need, the Apostle Paul instructs us in proper attitudes for obtaining and sustaining daily needs. "But godliness with contentment is great gain… And having food and raiment let us be therewith content" (1 Timothy 6:6, 8 KJV).

Wisdom shared by Solomon emphasizes both daily living and living daily. "So I concluded there is nothing better than to be happy and enjoy ourselves as long as we can. And people should eat and drink and enjoy the fruits of their labor, for these are gifts from God" (Ecclesiastes 3:12–13 NLT).

God's storehouse of mercy and love is the greatest source for obtaining these living essentials. "I have been young, and now am old; yet I have not seen the righteous forsaken, nor his seed begging bread" (Psalm 37:25 KJV). "Behold the eye of the Lord is upon them that fear him, upon them that hope in his mercy; To deliver their soul from death, and to keep them alive in famine" (Psalm 33:18–19 NLT).

Proper *shelter* in which to live is essential. God's concern for people has always been a place to live. God is a dynamic home builder. He built the first home for man in the garden: "And the Lord God planted a garden eastward in Eden, and there he put the man whom he had formed" (Genesis 2:8 KJV).

Jesus built for us a church home: "upon this rock I will build my church" (Matthew 16:18 KJV). Believers are called "brothers and sisters" in the Scripture. We are the family of God. "Ye are all the children of God by faith in Christ Jesus" (Galatians 3:26 KJV).

Jesus is away now building our heavenly home: "In my Father's house are many mansions: if it were not so, I would have told you. I go to prepare a place for you" (John 14:2 KJV).

The greatest blessing for a couple as they enter into marriage is to allow Christ to be the head and heart of their home. It takes three to make a happy home: a husband, a wife, and God. Only God can make their home complete. "Except the Lord build the house, they labor in vain that build it…" (Psalm 127:1a KJV).

There are over 550,000 homeless people in the United States. Some are runaways; others have been abandoned by their families. Some have lost their jobs, therefore, losing their homes through failed mortgages. Sadly enough, some have lost their homes through failed marriages. Many have chosen the nomadic lifestyle moving from place to place living in tents, under bridges, alleys, cardboard boxes, or homeless shelters.

God told Abraham to leave his country and to follow directions to a new land that would become his home. "Get thee out of thy country, and from thy kindred, and from thy father's house, unto a land that I will shew thee" (Genesis12:1 KJV). Abraham followed the Lord's word: "For he looked for a city which hath foundations, whose builder and maker is God" (Hebrews 11:10 KJV).

Abundant *strength* is needed for daily living. Courage and determination are important qualities to possess as we attempt to live daily. To assure happiness and success in living, we must develop physical endurance, moral fortitude, and deep spiritual convictions.

Personal discipline is required. "We are instructed to turn from godless living and sinful pleasures. We should live...with wisdom, righteousness, and devotion to God" (Titus 2:12 NLT).

Dependence upon God is an absolute necessity in daily living. "But Lord...be our strong arm each day and our salvation in times of trouble" (Isaiah 33:2 NLT). "The Lord is my rock, and my fortress, and my deliverer; my God, my strength, in whom I will trust..." (Psalm 18:2 KJV). "The Lord is the strength of my life; of whom shall I be afraid?" (Psalm 27:1 KJV).

An inti mate relationship with Christ is the perfect formula for daily living. "Abide in me, and I in you. As the branch cannot bear fruit of itself, except it abide in the vine; no more can ye, except ye abide in me" (John 15:4 KJV). As believers, Jesus is our life, and it's a wonderful life! "Without me ye can do nothing" (John 15:5c KJV).

"'I am come that they might have life, and that they might have life more abundantly" (John 10:10 KJV). Life, lots of life! Life that is full and overflowing. Life that is vibrant and enjoyable. It is life experienced daily! "This is the day" (Psalm 118:24 KJV).

The shepherd boy psalmist declared, "The Lord is my shepherd; I shall not want" (Psalm 23:1 KJV). An aged saint's testimony is "The Lord is my shepherd and *that's all I want!*"

Delight in obeying God's Word is imperative for daily living. "Delight thyself also in the Lord: and he shall give thee the desires of thine heart. Commit thy way unto the Lord; trust also in him; and he shall bring it to pass" (Psalm 37:4–5 KJV). "People do not live by bread alone; rather, we live by every word that comes from the mouth of the Lord" (Deuteronomy 8:3 NLT).

Submission to God in worship results in daily blessings and benefits. "Evening, and morning, and at noon, will I pray, and cry aloud: and he [God] shall hear my voice" (Psalm 55:17 KJV). "My voice shalt thou hear in the morning, O Lord; in the morning will I direct my prayer unto thee, and will look up" (Psalm 5:3 KJV). "Give unto the Lord the glory due unto his name; worship the Lord in the beauty of holiness… The Lord will give strength unto his people; the Lord will bless his people with peace" (Psalm 29:2, 11 KJV).

Daily living is to rely on the Lord's promises and to submit to his love and leadership. "So will I sing praise unto thy name for ever, that I may daily perform my vows" (Psalm 61:8 KJV).

"In the Morning"
Ralph Cushman

I met God in the morning,
When my day was at its best
And His presence came like sunrise,
Like a glory in my breast.

All day long the Presence lingered;
All day long He stayed with me;
And we sailed with perfect calmness
O'er a very troubled sea.

Living Every Day

Text: "And it came to pass in the seven and thirtieth year of the captivity of Jehoiachin king of Judah, in the twelfth month, on the seven and twentieth day of the month, that Evilmerodach king of Babylon in the year that he began to reign did lift up the head of Jehoiachin king of Judah out of prison; And he spake kindly to him, and set his throne above the throne of the kings that were with him in Babylon; And changed his prison garments: and he did eat bread continually before him all the days of his life. And his allowance was a continual allowance given him of the king, a daily rate for every day, all the days of his life" (2 Kings 25:27–30 KJV).

Biblical history records numerous occasions of God taking care of his people. The methods of God's assistance are manifold and miraculous. At times, he works through national leaders to help or to hinder in their journeys. God may use our friends and even our foes to accomplish his work. The experience recorded in this text is one such wonderful story.

Jehoiachin became king of Judah at the death of his father, Jehoiakim, in 598 BC. He was only eighteen years of age. He was inexperienced in the politics of the day. The only example of kingship he knew was his father who "did that which was evil in the sight of the Lord" (2 Kings 23:37 KJV). He was under the influence of his mother more than any other teacher or counselor in the kingdom. His mother was Nehushta (the brazen), the daughter of Elnathan, an influential prince of Jerusalem. Jehoiachin bore the resemblance of a "momma's boy," for the queen mother appears with him at all times in this scriptural biography.

Jehoiachin had no training in tactical warfare. He had never been in battle nor worn a soldier's armor. The scriptural record does not list any outstanding commander of Judah's army at this time. There was neither prophet nor counselor available to guide the young king. So when Nebuchadnezzar, the king of Babylon, sent troops to Jerusalem, Jehoiachin did not retaliate. He quietly and hurriedly surrendered himself and his kingdom. He only reigned as the king of Judah three months and was demoted from being king to a captive! "Nebuchadnezzar led King Jehoiachin away as a captive to Babylon" (2 Kings 24:15 NLT).

Jehoiachin was a prisoner in Babylon for thirty-seven years (598–560BC). During this time, Nebuchadnezzar died, and his son, Evil-Merodach, took over the throne. He possessed a higher regard for human life and foreign nobility than did his father. When he learned that the king of Judah had been a prisoner in Babylon for many years, he had him released and brought to the palace. There he treated Jehoiachin with compassion and dignity. He restored him to the ranks as a kingly counselor along with other exiled kings. He made arrangements for Jehoiachin to be cared for the remainder of his life. The concluding verses of 2 Kings describe his reward and restitution: "…and he did eat bread continually before the king all the days of his life. And his allowance was a continual allowance given him of the king, a *daily* rate, for *every day*, all the *days* of his life" (2 Kings 25:29–30 KJV, emphasis mine).

This historical record is a beautiful depiction of a believer in Christ. As sinners, we were held captive, locked away with no hope, until a new king came into our lives. King Jesus saved us from our captivity to sin and Satan. "If the Son therefore shall make you free, ye shall be free indeed" (John 8:36 KJV). Now, in Christ, we experience a wonderful new life with blessings beyond imagination!

Precious are the ingredients provided by the Lord for our living every day. We are granted the *king's approval*. As a prisoner, Jehoiachin had often been cursed, ridiculed, and mocked. He had been abandoned in the prison for thirty-seven years. Now the king shows him favor and compassion. "And he [the king] spake kindly to him" (2 Kings 25:28 KJV).

God is merciful and kind to all. "For his merciful kindness is great toward us" (Psalm 117:2 KJV). "Gracious is the Lord, and righteous; yea, our God is merciful" (Psalm 116:5 KJV).

God makes saints out of sinners. In Christ, we are no longer aliens but heirs of the kingdom of God. "Now therefore ye are no more strangers and foreigners, but fellowcitizens with the saints, and of the household of God" (Ephesians 2:19 KJV).

We live in *kingly accommodations.* Jehoiachin was released from prison and was given a room in the palace. "Evilmerodach king of Babylon in the year that he began to reign did lift up the head of Jehoiachin king of Judah out of prison" (2 Kings 25:27 KJV).

God has lifted us out of the pit and seated us in heavenly places! "'He brought me up also out of an horrible pit, out of the miry clay, and set my feet upon a rock" (Psalm 40:2 KJV). "And hath raised us up together, and made us sit together in heavenly places in Christ Jesus" (Ephesians 2:6 KJV).

What a wonderful transition for believers: from the pit to the palace! "In my father's house are many mansions… I go to prepare a place for you… I will come again, and receive you unto myself; that where I am, there ye may be also" (John 14:2–3 KJV).

Jehoiachin went from a life sentence in prison to a life sustained in the palace. "And his allowance was a continual allowance…all the days of his life" (2 Kings 25:30 KJV). A believer is given eternal life in Christ: "I give unto them eternal life; and they shall never perish" (John 10:28 KJV). We obtain "an inheritance incorruptible, and undefiled, and that fadeth not away, reserved in heaven for you, Who are kept by the power of God" (1 Peter 1:4-5a KJV).

For *living every day,* God dresses us in *kingly apparel.* As a prisoner of Babylon, Jehoiachin wore neither the crown of Judah nor the robe of royalty. Tattered rags were the garments of prisoners. But the king of Babylon gave him a new wardrobe: "and changed his prison garments" (2 Kings 25:29 KJV).

When the prodigal son returned home, the father replaced his rags with a robe and shoes and a ring signifying sonship. Believers in Christ have dropped the rags of sin and have donned the robes of righteousness in Christ. "If any man be in Christ, he is a new creature: old things are passed away; behold, all things are become new" (2 Cor. 5:17 KJV). "Ye have put off the old man with his deeds; And have put on the new man" (Colossians 3:9–10 KJV). "But put ye on the Lord Jesus Christ, and make not provision for the flesh" (Romans 13:14 KJV).

We develop a *kingly appetite* and are nourished with "soul food" in living every day. "And he did eat bread continually before him all the days of his life" (2 Kings 25:29 KJV). God cares for and he takes care of his people. "I have been young and now am old; yet have I not seen the righteous forsaken, nor his seed begging bread" (Psalm 37:25 KJV).

What a deli of delicious delicacies God prepares. God fed Moses manna in the dessert. Ravens brought fresh meat and bread to nourish Elijah. David described the banquet table which the Lord prepared for him. Jesus prepared breakfast for the disciples: "As soon then as they were come to land, they saw a fire of coals there, and fish laid thereon and bread… Jesus saith unto them, Come and dine" (John 21:9, 12 KJV).

To be "fed" by the Lord, all we need is an appetite for the things of God. "O taste and see that the Lord is good: blessed is the man that trusteth in him" (Psalm 34:8 KJV). "As newborn babes, desire the sincere milk of the word, that ye may grow thereby" (1 Peter 2:2 KJV).

John W. Peterson's words in the hymn: "Surely Goodness and Mercy," identify what *living every day* really means.

> He restoreth my soul when I'm weary;
> He giveth me strength day by day;
> He leads me beside the still waters;
> He guards me each step of the way.

And I will dwell in the house of the Lord forever,
And I will feast at His table spread for me;
Surely goodness and mercy shall follow me
All the days, all the days of my life.

And there was given unto him "a continual allowance given him of the king, *a daily rate, for every day, all the days of his life*" (2 Kings 25:30 KJV).

Really Living

TEXT: "I AM come that they might have life, and that they might have it more abundantly" (John 10:10b KJV). "My purpose is to give them a rich and satisfying life" (John 10:10 NLT).

The story is told of a wealthy Mississippi Delta farmer who purchased a new car. The car was the pride and enjoyment of his life and the talk of the town. He had it special ordered from the factory, gold trim inside and out, with all the bells, whistles, and accessories available. He kept it in immaculate condition, waxed and serviced, pampered like a baby. He loved the car so much until his request was to be buried in the car at his death.

When the man died, the family fulfilled his request. The funeral director placed his body in the driver's seat holding the steering wheel as if to drive off into eternity! At the cemetery a crane lifted the car up and lowered it into a deep grave. Two ole hired hands who had worked for him for many years watched at the gravesite. One remarked, "Now that's really living!"

Oh how confused we all are occasionally as to what constitutes "living!" Those who are successful in life may be living on "easy street." Those less fortunate are "moving toward the poor house." Some are living in the "fast lane," but in reality, they are getting nowhere fast!

A preacher friend's last church appointment was a four-year commission to Alaska. The cold, the snow, and the long periods of darkness were depressing. He retired to South Florida. His word to me from the warm sands of the sunny beach was "Now this, for me, is really living!"

There is a difference between "life" and "living." Creation is a beautiful picture of both life and living. "In the beginning God created the heavens and the earth. The earth was formless and empty, and darkness covered the deep waters…" (Genesis 1:1–2 NLT). That which God created was a life source. The potential for life was there, but no living organisms has yet existed. "Then God said, 'Let there be light,' and there was light…the land produced vegetation—all sorts of seed-bearing plants, and trees with seedbearing fruit" (Genesis 1:3, 12 NLT). Nothing lived until the life-rendering rays of light warmed the seedbeds of the earth. To a cold, dark, formless mass, God turned on the light, and life sprang up everywhere! "All things were made by him; and without him was not anything made that was made. In him was life; and the life was the light of men" (John 1:3–4 KJV).

To God, life is more than mere existence. Life is evolvement, development, growth, change, and productivity. The creation saga is expressed through four distinct and different sciences: geology, astrology, biology, and psychology. At first, God created the heavens and the earth and all the elements of the earth: the rocks, sand, dirt, minerals, and water. This became the seedbed for plant life to follow. In the soils of the earth were all the chemicals, nutrients, and ingredients needed for life to develop. It is no surprise then when we see plant life sprouting. "And the earth brought forth grass, and herb yielding seed after his kind, and the tree yielding fruit, whose seed was in itself, after his kind: and God saw that it was good" (Genesis 1:12 KJV).

Astrology was the next science God placed in motion. "And God said, Let there be lights in the firmament of the heaven to divide the day from the night; and let them be for signs, and for seasons, and for days, and years; And let them be for lights in the firmament of the heaven to give light upon the earth: and it was so. And God made two great lights; the greater light to rule the day, and the lesser light to rule the night: and he made the stars also" (Genesis 1:14–16 KJV).

Biology was brought into the creation with the appearance of living creatures. It must have been a fun day for the Lord as he began creating fish and fowl. Oh, what creativity and imagination went into this task!

Feathers and Plumes and Eider Down…
Some with Crops and some with Crowns.
With wings to fly and instinct to know,
When it's time to stay or time to go!
Bass in the lakes and trout in the streams
Each fulfills the anglers dreams!
Dolphins sing beneath the waves, And
Octopi sleep in hidden caves!
Feathers and fins, a nest or a shell…
Each has a story of creation to tell!

—Ralph Culp

"And God created great whales, and every living creature that moveth, which the waters brought forth abundantly, after their kind, and every winged fowl after his kind: and God saw that it was good" (Genesis 1:21).

Creation was now truly getting interesting. On the sixth day, God organized the earth into a wilderness wildlife habitat. He began by creating beasts for the forests, creatures for the jungles, and cattle for the fields. "God made the beast of the earth after his kind, and cattle after their kind, and everything that creepeth upon the earth after his kind: and God saw that it was good" (Genesis 1:25 KJV). The earth was now full of living creatures of God's design. They were to "be fruitful and multiply." They would produce offspring "of their kind" and of their image and likeness.

God is ready to advance to the next stage of creation, the science of psychology. God now creates a living being made in his image and likeness. One who possesses intellect and is able to express emotion. Beings that will live together in community and that can be trusted with responsibility and authority. A being with whom God can share fellowship. "So God created man in his own image, in the image of God created he him; male and female created he them. And God blessed them, and God said unto them, Be fruitful, and multiply, and replenish the earth, and subdue it: and have dominion over…every living thing that moveth upon the earth" (Genesis 1:27–28 KJV).

Man is the apex of God's creation. Man did not ascend from the animal kingdom; he is above it and separate from it. He is not a replica of reptile. Man is in the image of God. Upon creation, the animals became living creatures, but man became "a living soul" (Genesis 2:7 KJV). All the creatures have breath, but man has "the breath of life, the breath of God" (Genesis 2:7 KJV).

One of my respected seminary professors of years ago often quoted a little ditty, making light of the theory of evolution. It always brought smiles to serious students.

Once I was a tadpole beginning to begin. Then I was a frog with my tail tucked in! Then I became a monkey in a banana tree, but now I am a professor with a PhD!

We stand in awe at the Creator's interest in man. "When I look at the night sky and see the work of your fingers—the moon and the stars you set in place—what are mere mortals that you should think about them, human beings that you should care for them? Yet you made them only a little lower that God [Elohim] and crowned them with glory and honor. You gave them charge of everything you made, putting all things under their authority" (Psalm 8:3–6 NLT). God values every individual. His concern is unique. "The very hairs of your head are all numbered" (Matthew 10:30 KJV).

For evidence of life, a doctor listens for a heartbeat, checks for a pulse, or tests for a reflex. For evidence of being "really alive," we look for a gleam in one's eye, listen for laughter in their voice, and feel the warm touch of their hand in ours.

Living is more than gasping for air; it is grasping for adventures. It is more than existence; it is experience. Living is more than filling up an area of space; it is fulfilling an assignment. To be really alive is more than wishing upon a star; it is reaching for the stars. It is more than sitting on the bleachers; it is to be out on the field playing the game!

There was a very cautious man
Who never laughed or played
He never risked, he never tried,
He never sang or prayed.
And when one day he passed away
His insurance was denied,
For since he never really lived,
They claimed he never died!

—Anonymous

The purpose God has for man is to live life to the fullest, to be complete, competent, and content. The text reminds us that Jesus came that we might have life (be alive) and have life more abundantly (really live).

Life is tragic when a person has plenty to live on but nothing to live for! "A man's life consisteth not in the abundance of the things which he possesseth" (Luke 12:15 KJV). To know life is to know the Lord, to be blessed, and to know the One who blesses! "I am crucified with Christ: nevertheless I live; yet not I, but Christ liveth in me: and the life which I now live in the flesh I live by the faith of the Son of God, who loved me, and gave himself for me" (Galatians 2:20 KJV). For me to live is Christ..." (Philippians 1:21 KJV).

Now that's *really living*!

Alive in the Land of the Living

Text: "I will walk before the Lord in the land of the living" (Psalm 116:9 KJV).

"Yet I am confident I will see the Lord's goodness while I am here in the land of the living" (Psalm 27:13 NLT).

Fresh out of Egyptian bondage, the children of Israel followed Moses on a journey to the land God had promised the patriarchs. They were seeking for a new life in this "land of the living." The promise of God to Abraham concerning property for their homeland was granted to each succeeding generation. "And the Lord thy God will bring thee in the land which thy fathers possessed and thou shalt possess it and he will do thee good and multiply thee above thy fathers" (Deuteronomy 30:5 KJV).

This was to be a land of prosperity. God spoke to Moses at the burning bush a message of hope for his people in bondage. "I am come down to deliver them out of the hand of the Egyptians, and to bring them up out of that land unto a good and a large, land flowing with milk and honey"(Exodus 3:8 KJV).

In this "land of the living" God had assured them if they obeyed his commands, they would be royally blessed. "Your towns and your fields will be blessed. Your children and your crops will be blessed. The offspring of your herds and flocks will he blessed. Your fruit baskets and breadboards will be blessed. Wherever you go and whatever you do, you will be blessed" (Deuteronomy 28:3–6 NLT).

In this "land of the living," they would also be protected against diseases and defeats from their enemies. "If thou will diligently hearken to the voice of the Lord thy God, and wilt do that which is right in his sight, and wilt give ear to his commandments, and keep all his statues, I will put none of these diseases upon thee, which I have brought upon the Egyptians: for I am the Lord that healeth thee" (Exodus 15:26 KJV).

"None of these diseases." What a wonderful thought! Egypt was a land of disease and death. The ten plagues God brought upon the land because of Pharaoh's rebellion, all reeked of death. Egypt experienced death to their cattle. The river and all water sources turned to blood. Fish and all marine creatures died. The rotting carcasses washing ashore created other means of disease and death. The last and most severe plague was the death of the first born of every family including the first born of sheep, oxen, and cattle. Death! All around them was sorrow and grief!

The Egyptians were brilliant scientists and chemists. They had mastered the art of preservation of the body after death. Their technique of "mummifying" has yet to be equaled. They knew how to preserve the body but were dumfounded in the art of prolonging life. Many in Egypt died young. Various artifacts and relics found in archeological digs depict youth. King Tut was known as the "boy king." His wife, Ankhesenamun, was a young maiden. Their mummy casings give evidence of death while in their youth.

The children of Israel, however, had the blessing of life.

Genesis 5 reads like an extended record of birth certificates. In it are listed names, descendants, and years of life of every generation from Adam to Noah. Longevity was a blessing in each generation. Enoch was the youngest listed, yet he lived 365 years.

The years of the Egyptian sojourn were filled with the blessing of life. The plagues upon the land of Egypt did not come near the homes of the Israelites. They were safe and unharmed from these curses. Life was their greatest blessing.

As they left Egypt and were traveling through the wilderness, they became hungry, thirsty, and tired. They began to fear for their own lives. "And they said unto Moses, Because there were no graves in Egypt, hast thou taken us away to die in the wilderness?" (Exodus 14:11 KJV).

The people of Israel had the promise of life. "Honour thy father and thy mother, as the Lord thy God hath commanded thee; that thy days may be prolonged, and that it may go well with thee; in the land…" (Deuteronomy 5:16 KJV).

The patriarch Job experienced life and sorrows. He knew grief and woe. He bore pain and suffering. Yet he knew the promise of God. "Thou shalt come to thy grave in a full age" (Job 5:26 KJV). The record of his death indicates God's promise was fulfilled. "So Job died, being old and full of days" (Job 42:17 KJV). Job had lived a full life, and his life had been full!

Longevity was a comforting and satisfying truth to God's chosen people. They lived with the hope of life and blessings. "With long life will I satisfy him, and shew him my salvation" (Psalm 91:16 KJV). They prayed for their days to be exciting. "O satisfy us early with thy mercy; that we may rejoice and be glad all our days" (Psalm 90:14 KJV).

They enjoyed the blessings of life all through the years. "Lord, thou hast been our dwelling place in all generations" (Psalm 90:1 KJV). "I have been young, and now am old; yet have I not seen the righteous forsaken, nor his seed begging bread… The righteous shall inherit the land, and dwell therein forever" (Psalm 37:25, 29 KJV).

Life is God's specialty. Everything God formed, created, and touched came to life. "And the Lord God formed man of the dust of the ground, and breathed into his nostrils the breath of life; and man became a living soul" (Genesis 2:7 KJV).

The very purpose of Jesus coming into this world was to give man a new and different life. "And I give unto them eternal life; and they shall never perish…" (John 10:28 KJV).

Jesus identified himself as the very essence of life. "I am the way, the truth, and the life: no man cometh unto the Father, but by me" (John 14:6 KJV). He is the way; without him, there is no going. He is the truth; without him, there is no knowing. He is the life; without him, there is no living!

Jesus is life! He gives life! "In him was life; and the life was the light of men" (John 1:4 KJV). Lazarus died. Jesus restored him to living. In an even greater fashion, Jesus gives new life to sinners who are dead to God. "And you hath he quickened [brought to life], who were dead in trespasses and sins..." (Ephesians 2:1 KJV). The Scriptures provide a record of a believers spiritual DNA.

"This is the record that God hath given to us eternal life, and this life is in his Son. He that hath the Son hath life; and he that hath not the Son of God hath not life" (1 John 5:11–12 KJV).

Jesus is life! He is our life! He is the way to know and enjoy life. The Christian life is a glorious testimony for believers. A note often quoted is "Know Christ, know life. No Christ, no life." As a believer, I am alive in the land of the living, and Christ is alive in me! "For me to live is Christ..." (Philippians 1:21 KJV).

Living the Christian life is living by faith. "The life which I now live in the flesh I live by the faith of the Son of God, who loved me, and gave himself for me" (Galatians 2:20 KJV).

In the land of the living, our daily prayer and procedure is "so teach us to number our days, that we may apply our hearts unto wisdom" (Psalm 90:12 KJV). We are not to simply count the days but to make the days count, to be productive, and to live worthy of God's praise.

To be alive in the land of the living is to follow God's directions. The promise, as prescribed to ancient Israel, is equally binding on believers today.

> See, I have set before thee this day life and good, and death and evil. In that I command thee this day to love the Lord thy God, to walk in his ways, and to keep his commandments and his statutes and his judgments, that thou mayest live and multiply: and the Lord thy God shall bless thee in the land whither thou goest to possess it... I have set before you life and death, blessing and cursing: therefore choose life, that both thou and thy seed may live. (Deuteronomy 30:15–16, 19b KJV)

Alive in the land of the living! Let us live such a beautiful life so that when we die, even the undertaker will be sad to see us go!

Healthy Living

Text: "I will not make you suffer any of the diseases I sent on the Egyptians; for I am the Lord who heals you" (Exodus 15:26b NLT).

God blessed Egypt through Joseph's administration as the prime minister during the seven years of plenty. Seven years of famine would soon follow. When the draught famished all the food supplies in the surrounding nations, Joseph arranged for his father and seventy family descendants to move to Egypt in a section of land near the Nile Delta known as Goshen. "Joseph placed his father and his brethren, and gave them a possession in the land of Egypt, in the best of the land" (Genesis 47:11 KJV).

Dwelling in Egypt for over four hundred years, the children of Israel became a mighty nation of people. The first few years were pleasant and productive. After Joseph died, a new Pharaoh became ruler. He was harsh and mean toward the people of Israel. In fear of their number and strength, he made slaves of them. "So the Egyptians made the Israelites their slaves. They appointed brutal slave drivers over them...the Egyptians worked the people of Israel without mercy... They were ruthless in all their demands" (Exodus 1:11, 13, 14 NLT).

God used a series of ten plagues to punish Pharaoh and Egypt. Israel was miraculously protected from these harsh calamities. God blessed them with excellent health and prosperity. They watched as disease and death covered the land. They listened to the wails of grieving Egyptian families. They observed the destruction of the land

and of the people of Egypt until they were released to go to Canaan under Moses' leadership.

Israel was safely on their way to the land of promise when God made a covenant concerning their health and happiness. This covenant demanded that the people heed God's Word, obey his commands, and live righteous lives. God promised to bless and protect them spiritually and physically. They would not suffer the diseases of Egypt. He would be their Great Physician.

Moses reminded them of these diseases of Egypt.

> The Lord will strike you with wasting diseases, fever, and inflammation... These disasters will pursue you until you die... The Lord will afflict you with the boils of Egypt and with tumors, scurvy, and the itch, from which you cannot be cured. The Lord will strike you with madness, blindness, and panic...the Lord will overwhelm you and your children with indescribable plagues. These plagues will be intense and without relief, making you miserable and unbearably sick. He will afflict you with all the diseases of Egypt that you feared so much, and you will have no relief...the Lord will cause your heart to tremble, your eyesight to fail, and your soul to despair. (Deuteronomy 28:22, 27–28, 59–60, 65 NLT)

God is concerned with the health, happiness, and holiness of his people. God assures his people of life and health. The Ten Commandments awards a blessing for honoring parents: "that thy days may be long upon the land which the Lord thy God giveth thee" (Exodus 20:12 KJV).

This promise is often repeated throughout the Bible. "That thy days may be prolonged, and that it may go well with thee, in the land which the Lord thy God giveth thee" (Deuteronomy 5:16 KJV). The Apostle Paul quotes this passage to remind the Ephesian believers of one's Christian duty to parents. "That it may be well with thee, and that thou mayest live long on the earth" (Ephesians 6:3 KJV).

Genesis 5 is an account of the multicentenarian generations from Adam to Noah and are identified by the number of years lived and the names of their descendants. Enoch was the youngest with 365 years. The oldest was Enoch's son Methuselah who lived 969 years before he died. The epithet written about Abraham is a reminder that God keeps his promises concerning life. "Abraham lived for 175 years, and he died at a ripe old age, having lived a long and satisfying life. He breathed his last and joined his ancestors in death" (Genesis 25:7–8 NLT).

Healthy living incorporates the consumption of special foods for nutrition in a daily diet. Society today is weight conscious and deliberate in its attempts toward physical fitness. Diets and exercise programs are priorities for good health. Eager to lose weight, people tum to pills and powders, shakes and supplements, fads and fasts. They join gyms and frequent the spas for strenuous workouts of dance therapy, yoga, and aerobics for conditioning. A TV commercial recently aroused my attention: "Lose weight while you sleep!" *Wow*, I thought, *this idea may work for me!*

Proper nutritious diets are difficult to follow. The nervous system and the digestive system operate like Siamese twins. When I become nervous or anxious, I feel hungry. The craving grows stronger so I nibble on whatever snacks are available. Food that satisfy that gnawing hunger sensation when we are nervous is labeled comfort food. We eat to satisfy nerves, not nutrition—depression not diets.

"Ode to a Sandwich"
Ralph Culp

You can have a sandwich without cheese or ham,
without peanut butter or strawberry jam.
You can make a sandwich without mayo or spices, but
you can't make a sandwich without two slices!
You must have bread to make it complete,
rye or pumpernickel or white or wheat.

It doesn't really matter the grain or the spread
as long as you have two pieces of bread.

Leviticus 11 is a listing of forbidden and acceptable foods for Israel's wellbeing. Meats allowed for Israel included beef, fish, and fowl. Instructions are specific identifying what meats should not be eaten. Simple succulent delicacies were a delight for John the Baptist, a reclusive prophet ministering in the wilderness. "And his meat was locusts and wild honey" (Matthew 3:4 KJV).

God planted a garden with an abundant variety of vegetables and fruits. "And the Lord God planted a garden eastward in Eden; and there he put the man whom he had formed. And out of the ground made the Lord God to grow every tree that is pleasant to the sight, and good for food..." (Genesis 2:8–9 KJV).

God developed spices, herbs, and condiments to add flavor to man's food. The wheat fields produced grain for bread, the staple food for man's diet. Vineyards flowed with wine, and olive groves dripped with its precious oil. "He [God] causeth the grass to grow for the cattle, and herb for the service of man: that he may bring forth food out of the earth; And wine that maketh glad the heart of man, and oil to make his face to shine, and bread which strengthens man's heart" (Psalm 104:14–15 KJV).

Healthy living is more than emphasis upon the physical body. It also involves a positive attitude of faith and moral judgment. The disobedience of Adam and Eve brought a curse upon man. Every generation must now endure sorrows and debilitating difficulties as a result of their sinful choice. "When Adam sinned, sin entered the world. Adam's sin brought death, so death spread to everyone, for everyone sinned" (Romans 5:12 NLT).

As a result, the saints also get sick! John's prayer for Gaius, a sick saint, was "Beloved, I wish above all things that thou mayest prosper and be in health, even as thy soul prospereth" (3 John 2 KJV). "And even we believers also groan...for we long for our bodies to be released from sin and suffering" (Romans 8:23 NLT).

Healthy living is preventative and purposeful living. God gave "thou shalt not" instructions to prevent a lapse in obedience to his covenant. These directives provide a model for moral living as well as establishing good health practices. Faithfulness to God stimulates healthy living and results in fruitfulness in daily life.

Healthy living is free from injurious worldly contamination. "Love not the world, neither the things that are in the world. If any man love the world, the love of the Father is not in him... And the world passeth away and the lust thereof: but he that doeth the will of God abideth for ever" (1 John 2:15, 17 KJV).

Healthy living is easily observed through the tasteful decisions of the spiritually healthy individual. "Fix your thoughts on what is true, and honorable, and right, and pure, and lovely, and admirable. Think about things that are excellent and worthy of praise. Keep putting into practice all you learned and received from me... Then the God of peace will be with you" (Philippians 4:8–9 NLT).

The blessings of God, which make for healthy living, affects all areas of life.

"Bless the Lord, O my soul, and forget not all his benefits: Who forgiveth all thine iniquities [spiritual]; who healeth all thy diseases [physical]; Who redeemeth thy life from destruction [moral]; who crowneth thee with loving kindness and tender mercies [emotional]; Who satisfieth thy mouth with good things; so that thy youth is renewed [pleasurable]..." (Psalm 103:2–5 KJV).

Handicap Living

Text: "Peter said, 'I don't have any silver or gold for you. But I'll give you what I have. In the name of Jesus Christ the Nazarene, get up and walk!' Then Peter took the lame man by the right hand and helped him up. And as he did, the man's feet and ankles were instantly healed and strengthened. He jumped up, stood on his feet, and began to walk! Then, walking, leaping, and praising God, he went into the Temple with them" (Acts 3:6–8 NLT).

The first recorded apostolic miracle is the healing of a "man lame from his birth." During the Bible days, it was not uncommon to find people in this condition. "Now there is at Jerusalem by the sheep market a pool…called Bethesda, having five porches. In these lay a great multitude of impotent folk, of blind, halt, withered…" (John 5:2–3 KJV).

Statistics for handicap/disability living are staggering. Over forty million Americans face life with some type of disability. The average is one in four adults.

An individual is more than a body of muscle and flesh. He is also personality, emotion, wit, and wisdom. Some suffer disabilities in the body, limited in strength and endurance. Others struggle with emotional storms, which drown them in fears, anxiety, or rage. We must view these as a person with a disability rather than as a disabled person.

We sometimes confuse a handicap with a disability. A disability is a condition which restricts one's ability to function physically, emotionally, mentally, or socially. A handicap is something immaterial that interferes with or delays action or progress. A handicap may be referred to as a deterrent, hindrance, snag, or setback. One may slip on an icy walkway and break a leg. He wears a cast and is on crutches for a few days. He may be unable to complete his normal tasks and to participate in other activities, but this is only a temporary condition. He is handicapped from his regular routines, but he is not disabled from doing his work.

Whether one has a permanent disability or a limitation from a handicap, attitude is the key to a successful coping experience.

What may be accomplished does not depend on the disability but on the person with the disability.

Faith in God is our greatest source of help. An inner strength can be more powerful than muscle strength. "We can rejoice, too, when we run into problems and trials, for we know that they help us develop endurance. And endurance develops strength of character, and character strengthens our confident hope of salvation" (Romans 5:3–4 NLT).

If a disability limits you, don't give up—push life to that limit. Go as far as you can, as hard as you can, as long as you can! If the disability is rigid, become flexible. Being able to "give and take, bend but don't break" works in most situations of life.

Determination is a valuable asset. Difficult adventures in our daily grind can be lessened through a determined commitment to overcome. Benjamin Franklin is credited with saying, "Diligence overcomes difficulties."

The children's fairytale *The Hare and the Tortoise* illustrates this principle. The tortoise was heavier, slower, older, not as agile nor as capable as the hare, but he was determined. He kept going. He was willing to stick his neck out and do his best in the only way he knew. He didn't give up!

A fellow student during college days walked with a severe limp.

His right arm was deformed and without strength. He could not converse for stuttering. He felt that God had called him to preach, but he was greatly limited from proclaiming a sermon. However, he could sing like a canary. He did not give in to his limitation. He was disabled, but he was not handicapped!

If your handicap is stress and you are struggling to "keep it together," don't boil over; turn down the heat! Identify the source of stress. Briefly distance yourself from that stress issue if possible. Take a personal break. Go for a walk. Learn to relax.

Redirecting your energy will recharge your emotional battery.

Being "calm, cool, and collected" is more appealing than being "angry, anxious, and aggravated."

Stress, if uncontrolled, can lead to much more serious and severe disorders. Phobias of all types can develop. More than a third of all adults experience panic attacks. Learning to depend on God for calmness and strength is of utmost importance.

During his earthly ministry, Jesus encountered many cases of disabled and handicapped persons. Some were visually impaired. Bartimaeus (Mark 10:46) and the man born blind (John 9) are two examples. Both received a miracle of sight from Jesus. Many witnesses to these miracles refused to believe the authority demonstrated by Jesus. They chose to remain "spiritually blind" rather than see the truth. To live in suspicion and doubt is a handicap as great as the visual disability!

Healing physical disabilities were unique miracles for Jesus. Four men brought a paralyzed man to Jesus (Mark 2). We are not told the extent of his paralysis. We do know that he could not walk and depended on family and friends for assistance. He was blessed to have friends who cared.

Another invalid person lay on his mat by the pool of Bethesda.

He had been sick and waiting for a miracle for thirty-eight years. When Jesus asked if he would like to be healed, his answer was a dismal word of discouragement: "I can't, sir, for I have no one to put me into the pool when the water bubbles up. Someone else always gets there ahead of me" (John 5:7 NLT). Not only was he disabled and could not do for himself, he was handicapped for he had no one to care for him!

The healing of emotionally and mentally disabled individuals was a specialty of the Great Physician. Demon possession was common in those days. Those possessed persons experienced emotional trauma, physical limitations, and spiritual depression.

The story of one demon-possessed man demonstrates a violent and debilitating condition. He is possessed by an evil spirit that won't let him talk. "Whenever this spirit seizes him, it throws him violently to the ground. He foams at the mouth, gnashes his teeth and becomes rigid...it has [the spirit] often thrown him into the fire or water to kill him" (Mark 9:17–18, 22 NLT).

Many Bible characters struggled through life with a major handicap. Moses had a speech impediment. "And Moses said, O my Lord, I am not eloquent... I am slow of speech, and of a slow tongue" (Exodus 4:10 KJV).

King Saul possessed a violent temper and was given to fits of rage. "Saul [became] very angry...kept a jealous eye on David. A tormenting spirit overwhelmed Saul, and he began to rave in his house like a madman" (1 Samuel 18:8–10 NLT).

Jonathan's son, Mephibosheth, was lame as a child from an accident. At age five, his grandfather Saul and his father Jonathan were killed in battle. When the child's nurse heard the news, she picked him up and ran for safety to spare his life. But as she hurried away, she dropped him, and he became crippled. (Related in 2 Samuel 4).

The Apostle Paul suffered from a handicap affecting him in body, mind, and spirit. "I was given a thorn in the flesh [physical], a messenger from Satan to torment me [spiritual] and keep me from becoming proud [emotional]" (2 Corinthians 12:7 NLT).

Job was a man of great faith, yet his testimony is a heart cry of misery. "And now my life seeps away. Depression haunts my days. At night my bones are filled with pain, which gnaws at me relentlessly" (Job 30:16–17 NLT).

Every person will face some physical or emotional handicap or disability during their lifetime. It may only be a slight limitation, or it could be a major liability.

The greatest disability in life is of a spiritual nature. Like the lame man in the text, we are born with major issues as if to be lame from birth. God calls it the sin nature. We are spiritually helpless to correct this problem. "As it is written, There is none righteous, no, not one...there is none that seeketh after God... For all have sinned and come short of the glory of God" (Romans 3:10–11, 23 KJV).

Man must look to God for salvation. He alone can give us a miracle of healing and hope. Only in Christ will we find peace and forgiveness. In the name of Jesus, like the lame man, we can be lifted up and go running and leaping through life to worship God.

Clean Living

Text: "And there came a leper to him, beseeching him, and kneeling down to him, and saying unto him, If thou wilt, thou canst make me clean. And Jesus, moved with compassion, put forth his hand, and touched him, and saith unto him, I will; be thou clean. And as soon as he had spoken, immediately the leprosy departed from him, and he was cleansed" (Mark 1:40–42 KJV).

Of the many diseases during the Bible days, leprosy was the most dreaded and serious of all. There was no known cure, and no balm eased the pain. A leper was doomed to a miserable life and a horrible death unless a divine miracle occurred.

A leper was hideous to look upon. The ugly appearance was repulsive. In extreme cases, scabs and sores covered the entire body. A bloody pus drained from open lesions. The odor of rotting flesh emanated from these sores. White spots covered the body, and hair fell out in patches. Sometimes leprosy progressed to the point that feet or hands would drop off.

The disease was contagious; whoever came in contact with the leper was defiled. The leper was doomed to a homeless life of poverty. The laws regulating health and cleanliness were specific.

> The priest shall pronounce the leper utterly unclean…the leper in whom the plague is, his clothes shall be rent, and his head bare, and he shall put a covering upon his upper lip, and shall cry, Unclean, unclean. All the days wherein the

plague shall be in him he shall be defiled; he is unclean: he shall dwell alone…(Leviticus 13:44–46 KJV)

The healing miracles of Jesus were accompanied with words of assurance to those who had been healed. "And he [Jesus] said unto her, Daughter, thy faith hath made thee whole; go in peace, and be whole of thy plague" (Mark 5:34 KJV).

Since the lepers were declared to be unclean, Jesus also gave words of assurance concerning their cleansing. Jesus said to the leprous man, "I will; be thou clean" (Mark 1:41 KJV).

A distinction in words is used for healing from "made whole" to "cleansed." Jesus healed the sick; they were made whole. He cleansed the lepers. A man with a withered hand was healed. "He [Jesus] said unto the man, Stretch forth thy hand…and his hand was restored whole as the other" (Luke 6:10 KJV). Ten lepers cried to Jesus for mercy: "and he said to them, Go show yourselves unto the priests… as they went, they were cleansed" (Luke 17:14 KJV).

Leprosy was a defilement of the flesh. Living in filth, a leper's clothes were ragged and dirty. When in public places, the leper was to continually cry out "unclean" so others could avoid him.

The greatest hope for a leper was to one day be clean and accepted among the people.

Words of hope from the lips of Jesus fell upon the ears of the leper. He had not asked for healing but for cleansing. "Thou canst make me clean." Jesus did not respond with words of healing but with "be thou clean." To be healed was to be cleansed: "the leprosy departed from him and he was cleansed."

Like leprosy, sin has marred every detail of man's life. Isaiah shares God's plea with his people who have rebelled against him. "Ah sinful nation, a people laden with iniquity, a seed of evildoers, children that are corrupters: they have forsaken the Lord, they have provoked the Holy One of Israel unto anger, they are gone away backward" (Isaiah 1:4 KJV).

Isaiah describes how sin affects each person "…the whole head is sick, and the whole heart faint. From the sole of the foot even unto the head there is no soundness in it; but wounds, and bruises, and putrifying sores" (Isaiah 1:5–6 KJV).

God offers to man a remedy for this "sin plague." It is to be cleansed.

> Wash you, make you clean; put away the evil of your doings from before mine eyes; cease to do evil... Come now, and let us reason together, saith the Lord: though your sins be as scarlet, they shall be as white as snow; though they be red like crimson, they shall be as wool. (Isaiah 1:16, 18 KJV)

David under the burden of his sins cried out for mercy. Sin had made him dirty, ugly, and despised. He asked God for cleansing. "Wash me thoroughly from mine iniquity, and cleanse me from my sin... Purge me with hyssop, and I shall be clean: wash me, and I shall be whiter than snow... Create in me a clean heart, O God" (Psalm 51:2, 7, 10 KJV).

How wonderful the salvation available in Jesus! God not only forgives our sins, he washes and makes us clean. God removes the penalty and the pain of guilt when we seek his forgiveness. "The blood of Jesus Christ...cleanseth us from all sin" (1 John 1:7 KJV).

"Nothing but the Blood"
Robert Lowry

What can wash away my sin?
Nothing but the blood of Jesus!
What can make me whole again?
Nothing but the blood of Jesus!

Oh! Precious is the flow
That makes me white as snow;
No other fount I know,
Nothing but the blood of Jesus.

A comparative description of God's mercy: A child comes in from playing in the rain. He is covered with mud from head to toe. His mother says, "Oh my! How dirty! Go wash your hands, and mother will love you!"

God looks at sinners, all covered with sin from the world's mud holes and says, "I love you. Now go wash your face!"

"God showed his great love for us by sending Christ to die for us while we were still sinners" (Romans 5:8 NLT).

Even though the leper has been cleansed and offerings have been made with the priests satisfying the law's requirements, his identity is a leper. "Now when Jesus was in Bethany, in the house of Simon the leper" (Matthew 26:6 KJV). This Simon is identified as "the leper" to distinguish him from other Simons in the Bible narratives: Simon Peter, Simon the Zealot, and Simon the tanner.

Reputation always follows a person. The Apostle Paul referred to himself as a sinner, even after his glorious salvation experience. "Christ Jesus came into the world to save sinners; of whom I am chief" (1 Timothy 1:15 KJV). A saint is a sinner saved by grace!

As believers in Christ, we have been washed from our sins. "But ye are washed, but ye are sanctified, but ye are justified in the name of the Lord Jesus" (1 Corinthians 6:11 KJV).

However, we are still in the flesh with its many appetites and limitations. Temptation is still very real, and the flesh is prone to sin. Paul shared his struggles in the flesh. "And I know that nothing good lives in me, that is, in my sinful nature…if I do what I don't want to do…it is sin living in me" (Romans 7:18, 20 NLT). John reminds believers, "If we say that we have no sin, we deceive ourselves…" (1 John 1:8 KJV).

It is impossible for one to live a sinless life, but we are to "sin less" as we mature as Christians. We are to seek for purity and cleanliness in our Christian behavior. "Blessed are the pure in heart: for they shall see God" (Matthew 5:8 KJV).

God's desire for believers is "that we should be holy and without blame before him in love" (Ephesians 1:4 KJV). We are encouraged to live clean lives. "Let not sin therefore reign in your mortal body" (Romans 6:12 KJV).

Since this is God's expectation for believers, we should strive to please him. How can we do this? An ole adage is correct which says, "Cleanliness is next to *godliness*!" For good physical health, cleanliness is a must. The Health Department inspects restaurants regularly for cleanliness in the kitchen. An epidemic of E. coli can spread rapidly from unwashed hands of restaurant employees.

Signs are posted in public restrooms urging users to "wash their hands." Hospitals and clinics conveniently display antibacterial soap dispensers so everyone can have clean hands.

Good spiritual health also depends on cleanliness. Believers are commanded to maintain clean moral living. "Pure religion and undefiled before God…is…to keep himself unspotted from the world" (James 1:27 KJV). "Cleanse your hands, ye sinners, and purify your hearts…" (James 4:8 KJV).

The best way to stop the spread of a disease is simply to keep away from the contamination. The same is true spiritually. "Touch not, taste not, handle not" (Colossians 2:21 KJV). "Be ye separate, saith the Lord, and touch not the unclean thing" (2 Corinthians 6:17 KJV).

When there is sin in our lives, we must confess it to the Lord and seek his forgiveness (cleansing) immediately. "If we confess our sins, he is faithful and just to forgive us our sins, and to cleanse us from all unrighteousness" (1 John 1:9 KJV).

"Since you have heard about Jesus and have learned the truth that comes from him, throw off your old sinful nature and your former way of life, which is corrupted by lust and deception. Instead let the Spirit renew your thoughts and attitudes. Put on your new nature, created to be like God—truly righteous and holy" (Ephesians 4:21–24 NLT).

The psalmist asked, "Who shall ascend into the hill of the Lord? or who shall stand in his holy place?" (Psalm 24:3 KJV). The answer is an awesome reminder for clean living. "He that hath clean hands, and a pure heart" (v4).

May our prayer and ultimate desire be "Create in me a clean heart, O God…" (Psalm 51:10 KJV).

Circumstantial Living

TEXT: "WE ARE pressed on every side by troubles, but we are not crushed. We are perplexed, but not driven to despair. We are hunted down, but never abandoned by God. We get knocked down, but we are not destroyed. Through suffering, our bodies continue to share in the death of Jesus so that the life of Jesus may also be seen in our bodies" (2 Corinthians 4:8–10 NLT).

Uncle Jesse, faithful ole Uncle Jesse! Sometimes he's there when you need him, always he's there when you don't need him! As an army war veteran, he's eager to share stories from the battlefield. Though you have heard these stories many times before, they seem to be more exciting each time he relates the experience…at least exciting to him.

Uncle Jesse grew up during the Great Depression era of the 1920s. He reminisces about the good ole days, yet he describes in vivid detail how hard it was to eke out a living. Plowing the fields with a pair of stubborn mules, taking a bath in a #2 washtub and drinking water from the well in a gourd dipper are among his favorite stories.

Church services on Sunday would not be the same without Uncle Jesse. He makes his way down the side aisle to a corner seat on the second pew from the front. "That's my seat," he snorts, if you happen to be sitting in that pew.

It has become a practice among other church goers not to ask Uncle Jesse how he is feeling because he will tell you! "This ole hip is gonna go out on me one of these days." "My knees were so stiff I can hardly walk." "It must have been those onions I ate for supper; my gut growled and rolled all night."

Everyone waits for his usual concluding words: "I'm just ole and wore out; ain't good for nothing anymore, but I am in pretty good shape for the shape I am in. Under the circumstances I'm gonna make it a while longer!"

"Under the circumstances." This is the road most people are traveling. Life doesn't always turn out the way we had hoped. Unexpected things happen. Cherished plans get altered. A normal life seems almost impossible, for we never know from one day to the next what surprises may come our way.

Circumstantial living is not planning out your life but living out your life when your plans fail. It is to initiate "plan B." Everyone should be allowed to dream dreams of successful living, dreams which foster hope in an underprivileged environment. Dreams of fame and fortune, of duty and discipline should cause a person to reach for the stars and not give up in the face of failure.

Dreams however are often shattered. The "make-believe" world of a child gives way to a "hard to believe" world of an adult. The "boy wonder" grows up to become a "man blunder." The "little princess" will trade in her tiara for a hardhat and safety glasses.

Just like our dreams, life is often shattered. We find ourselves living, not as we had planned, but under the circumstances of life's new challenges.

Paul and his missionary team encountered numerous roadblocks and took many detours in finding the place of service God had planned for them. They traveled through the areas of Phrygia and Galatia being prevented from preaching the Gospel in the province of Asia at that time. Coming to the borders of Mysia, they turned north for the province of Bithynia. Again Paul felt the Holy Spirit would not allow them to go further. Seeking the approving leadership of the Holy Spirit, they traveled on through Mysia to the seaport city of Troas. That night, Paul, in a vision, heard a man from Macedonia praying, pleading for him to "come over into Macedonia and help us" (Acts 16:9b K.JV).

Luke in relating this experience explains how the missionary team adapted to circumstantial living. "And after he had seen the vision, immediately we endeavored to go into Macedonia, assuredly gathering that the Lord had called us for to preach the gospel unto them" (Acts 16:10 KJV).

These servants of the Lord were anxious to preach the Gospel. They also knew that everyone needed to hear this word. But they were committed to following the leadership of the Holy Spirit. For "eager beavers," it is almost impossible to wait. To postpone, to cancel, or to delay a needed event is difficult to do. But we learn that in every occupation delays come, detours cannot be avoided, and dangers often are prevalent in accomplishing our tasks.

It is often noted that things turn out best for people who make the best of the way things turn out. Living with our circumstances is much more profitable than living under the circumstances.

Taking control of our unfortunate situations is better than being controlled by these difficulties.

Learning to live in harmony with life's heartaches paves the way to victory over life's hurts. Dolly Parton said, "If you want the rainbow, you gotta put up with the rain." On a return trip through Iconium and Antioch, Paul exhorted the believers to continue in the faith because "we must suffer many hardships to enter the Kingdom of God" (Acts 14:22b NLT).

It's those "hardships" that make circumstantial living necessary.

Marie Osmond shared her philosophy for the tough times: "Life can be real tough…you can either learn from your problems, or keep repeating them over and over."

The prophet Habakkuk saw tough times ahead for the nations. In their rebellion and immorality, judgment was sure to come. As he faced the trials of future failures, he expressed hope through the circumstances of his life.

"Although the fig tree shall not blossom, neither shall fruit be in the vines; the labor of the olive shall fail, and the fields shall yield no meat; the flock shall be cut off from the fold, and there shall be no herd in the stalls; Yet, I will rejoice in the Lord. I will joy in the God of my salvation" (Habakkuk 3:17–18 KJV).

Following the miracle of feeding the 5000, Jesus sent the disciples away assuring them that he would rejoin them on the other side of the sea. It was late afternoon when the men entered a ship to cross the Sea of Galilee. During the night, a violent storm arose. Gale force winds ripped the sails and drenched the tiny ship as tidal waves lapped over the brow. In great fear, even the bravest of the brave cried out to God for mercy.

Knowing of their peril and panic, Jesus came to their rescue. Through the flashes of lightening, the men saw a figure coming toward them walking on the water. Their fears intensified. What a relief in recognizing the voice of Jesus who cried out to them, "Be of good cheer; it is I; be not afraid" (Matthew 14:27 KJV).

In bold excitement, Peter asked if he could come to meet the Lord on the water. Jesus invited him to come. In an instant, Peter was over the side of the ship and into the water walking to Jesus. When Peter looked and evaluated the circumstances surrounding him, he began to sink. Immediately Jesus reached out and lifted him up and back into the ship.

This experience of Peter is a lesson for us in circumstantial living. In the midst of life's storms, when we are at our lowest ebb, when terrors frighten us into a panic, when we have lost all hope, when we have exhausted all resources available, Jesus comes to us walking on the water. That which was over the head of Peter was under the feet of Jesus. All of life's problems, snags, and detours are under the control of the Lord.

Peter took his eyes off of the Lord and began looking at the storm. He was more captivated by the storm's gusts than by the Savior's grace. His thought must have been, "Well, under the circumstances, looks like I am going to drown." Jesus walks on top of all circumstances. He changes the direction of winds that blow against us. He calms the waves of apprehension and opposition. He lifts us from beneath to safety on high.

Life changes daily. Circumstances may alter our course, but we must not falter in courage. Jesus asked, "Wherefore didst thou doubt?" (Matthew 14:31 KJV). Regardless of what may happen in life, do not lose hope. Do not faint, falter, nor fail. Turn the circumstances into a challenge. If life gives you lemons, make lemonade. Above all else, keep your eyes on Jesus.

"I have set the Lord always before me: because he is at my right hand, I shall not be moved" (Psalm 16:8 KJV).

Conclusion

"AND NOW FOR the rest of the story" are the introductory words Paul Harvey used to conclude his weekly radio messages. His stories of inspiration and courage brought hope to everyone.

"And now, for the rest of Becky's story!" The procedures followed by the medical staff at the cancer clinic were rigorous and thorough. There would be radical surgery to remove the tumors and other cancer-infected tissue. There would be a treatment each month for twenty-four months. The doctors were confident these treatments would preserve her life for the duration of this time and perhaps some extended months. Two days were needed for each treatment. The chemo used, while destroying the cancer, had debilitating effects on her body. She experienced tremendous weight gain, loss of hair, fatigue, edema, weakness, excruciating pain, and emotional trauma during this procedure.

Once the surgery was complete, the treatments began. Before each treatment, blood work to determine the T cell count and intravenous Benadryl was administered. When Becky went for the eighteenth treatment, the T cell count had multiplied tremendously over the previous month. Hurriedly the doctor performed several other tests to determine the level of cancer growth. Conferring with others in the medical team, he decided to stop all treatments.

The time was November, just before the Thanksgiving Day holidays. The doctor said, "We will not do a treatment today. Go home and enjoy with family, as best you can, the holiday season."

Before leaving the parking garage, Becky remarked, "He did not give us a return appointment. Please go back to the office and schedule a date for after Christmas."

She remained in the car while I went back to the office. Once there, the doctor explained. "I do not think there will be a need for a return appointment. She will probably not live through this time."

I shared this word with Becky. She sat quiet for a few moments.

With her head bowed, her lips moved in silent prayer to God.

Finishing her prayer, she patted me on the knee, smiled beautifully, and said, "Let's go home. We have cooking and shopping to do for the holidays!"

During the following months, many unusual experiences occurred. At a time when the doctors said she was dying, she was living to the max. She pushed each day to keep going. She planned outings, and trips, and parties for friends. She baked birthday cakes and painted ceramic gifts for grandchildren. She began teaching a Bible class at church for special needs adults. There seemed to be no stopping to her even in a wheelchair with portable oxygen.

As pastor, caring for grieving families is time-consuming and emotionally tiring. For the next several months, even years, after Becky was thought to be dying, she accompanied me in caring for many of these families. Fifty two church members and nine persons of our family would die during this time. Many of these, Becky sat by their hospital bed and held their hand as they slipped into eternity in death. Truly amazing! Patients and families were greatly blessed by her presence and love.

After some time, we made an appointment with the cancer doctor. He was shocked and thrilled to see her. She asked him to perform all the tests again. The result: No evidence of cancer anywhere! God had truly performed a marvelous miracle. She lived thirteen years past the time the doctors were assured she would die and died from other complications, cancer free.

Becky understood that God had extended her life for a special ministry purpose. She fulfilled that purpose.

"All praise to God, the Father of our Lord Jesus Christ. God is our merciful Father and the source of all comfort. He comforts us in all our troubles so that we can comfort others. When they are troubled, we will be able to give them the same comfort God has given us" (2 Corinthians 1:3–4 NLT).

God may not perform many of his marvelous wonders until… "The Saints Also Get Sick!"

About the Author

SURVIVING THE EBB and flow of life, often flooding a minister's family, prepared Ralph Culp as an inspirational writer to readers of all ages. Educational training with a Master of Ministries degree in biblical studies and Doctor of Ministries degree in pastoral counseling enhanced his ability to write with compassion and confidence.

As pastor for fifty-seven years, Dr. Culp consoled the bereaving, comforted the sick, and counseled individuals from brokenness to wholeness. Compassion for the hurts of others deepened as he cared for his wife during an extended illness and death.

In writing, as in his preaching, Dr. Culp paints pictures of hope and happiness. Now retired, Ralph finds fulfillment as a freelance speaker and writer. Camping and hiking mountain trails are favorite enjoyments.

CPSIA information can be obtained
at www.ICGtesting.com
Printed in the USA
BVHW032038250421
605822BV00006B/175